I0689685

THE TEMPLE MOUNTAIN CAFE

THE TEMPLE MOUNTAIN CAFE

CHINLE MILLER

Yellow Cat
PUBLISHING

Copyright © 2021 by Chinle Miller/Yellow Cat Publishing™

All rights reserved, including the right of reproduction in whole or in part in any form. Yellow Cat and the accompanying logo are registered trademarks owned by Yellow Cat Publishing. www.yellowcatbooks.com. Any resemblance to actual persons, living or dead, or events is entirely coincidental.

Cover by Cary Cox. End photo of the Chocolate Drops in the Maze is a stock photo licensed from Shutterstock.

For Lonnie
And for W.E.B., inventor of the Shumway Latte

CONTENTS

1

Bud Shumway sat on a sandstone cliff high above the Green River, feet dangling over the edge while shading his eyes from the glaring sun, musing on how warm it was for early November in the canyon country of southeastern Utah.

He'd seen more than one late autumn where the snows would've prevented him from even getting out to the rim, some six or seven miles south of the town of Green River, and he knew the dry winter was because it was a La Niña year. In any case, he was enjoying being able to get out.

Actually, he was conflicted about the matter, not sure if he should be enjoying the lack of snow, as he knew the moisture was what kept the soils from blowing away in the spring winds, soils that were needed for the melons he grew on his farm out on Long Street. But he enjoyed being able to get out into the backcountry, an area that seemed to stretch forever and that he called the Big Empty.

Bud swung his legs a little, feeling a sense of bravado, half-hanging over the rim. He was actually afraid of heights, and even sitting there was a bit unsettling, even though he knew he couldn't fall, as there was a wide shelf just a few feet below him that wasn't visible from behind, his feet almost touching it.

He laughed, thinking back to the time he and his wife, Wilma Jean, had come out there, and she'd taken a picture of him dangling his feet in this same spot, later putting it in his "Best of Bud" annual calendar that she sent to friends and family. His Aunt Rhoda had called him later and chewed him out, saying he had others to think of and shouldn't be so cavalier about his safety. Bud had tried to tell her he'd been in no danger, but she wouldn't listen, reminding him of all the crazy things he'd done in his youth, which he'd rather not be reminded of.

Now studying the river far below, Bud felt enough vertigo that he finally had to get up and go lean on the green Toyota Land Cruiser with the sheriff's emblem on its side, even though he was in no danger of falling.

Bud was not only a melon farmer, but was also Sheriff of Emery County, Utah. He'd come out the River Road to check out a report of something strange called in by Sammy, who ran the Green River Airport, such as it was, consisting of only a hanger, a runway, a windsock, and a few lights, though Bud wasn't sure what else an airport that saw a plane maybe every other day would need.

Sammy had said he'd seen an odd aircraft, describing it merely as a large flying tripod with a big bubble on top. Bud had asked if it was a UFO, but Sammy had been reluctant to call it that, even though he couldn't identify what it actually was. It was broad daylight, so Bud knew Sammy wasn't imagining it, especially since he not only was a straight shooter but was probably the most unlikely person on the planet to see a UFO, since he claimed to not believe in them.

Sammy had told him the aircraft had gone toward the river, so Bud had quickly grabbed his camera and headed down the River Road. Even though he didn't think he had much of a chance of seeing anything, he always enjoyed getting out into the backcountry, especially if he could say it was job related.

Now seeing something in the far distance, way above Horse Bench, he grabbed his binoculars from the seat of the Cruiser, but by the time he got them focused, it was gone.

Probably just a small aircraft, Bud mused, maybe even his wife's

Cessna, though he was pretty sure she didn't have any airdrops planned, as it was too late in the year for supplying rafters and mountain bikers. Besides, hadn't she said something about her cafe, the Melon Rind, catering lunch for the Shriner's Club today?

Wondering what they were having, Bud now scanned the landscape below, his stomach beginning to feel empty. The candycane stripes of the Brushy Basin Morrison badlands shone in the bright sun, the greens and yellowish-browns making the hills look like giant layer cakes butting up against the sheer reddish-brown cliffs of the Cedar Mountain Formation.

Far below, the deep green of the river cut through it all like a shiny snake winding its way on downstream into lands untouched and unknown to all but the ancient dinosaur bones buried in layer after layer of dino graveyards.

Now a flash down by the river caught Bud's eye, and he trained his binoculars far below. There, much to his surprise, were what looked to be three—no, four—boats beached along the water, and he could make out a number of tiny figures nearby.

Few floated the river this time of year, Bud mused, for in a normal year it would be starting to freeze up. In fact, at this same time just last year, he'd received a call from some rafters in nearby Desolation Canyon who, when they'd started out, had open water, but after a couple of days, the river had frozen almost solid between both banks, making it impossible for them to proceed.

He'd had to initiate a helicopter rescue, and the rafters were forced to leave all their gear behind. The spring floods had later carried most of it away, though a couple of coolers had survived, coming aground near town, the cans of drinks inside having exploded from the cold.

Noting that the rafts were all dark brown, Bud wondered if it weren't a party of geologists or someone doing some kind of research, for most recreational river runners had colorful rafts—yellow or red. But as he looked closer, he could tell he wasn't looking at rafts at all, but rather what appeared to be some kind of wooden dories, the types used years ago.

To his knowledge, nobody used wooden dories these days, except maybe down in the Grand Canyon, where Martin Litton had introduced them years before. Thinking back, he recalled that there was one in the Green River Museum, the dory used by the legendary Bert Loper, who knew the Green and Colorado rivers like the back of his hand and had died rafting the Colorado at the age of 79.

Or had it belonged to the even more legendary Kolb brothers, who predated Loper? Maybe he and Wilma Jean should go revisit the museum, Bud thought, as it had been awhile.

Noting that the group along the river was now pitching their tents as if to stay overnight, Bud could see a yellow raft coming along the river, floating on by the camp, appearing to have five or six people on board. This looked more like a day outing, he thought, someone floating on down to Mineral Bottom, where they would be picked up by a shuttle from Radium. He knew a group that large would need a second raft for their gear if they were camping.

Watching as the yellow raft disappeared around the bend, Bud could now see two figures in the rocks above the camp. He watched for awhile, but they seemed to just be sitting there, doing nothing, though he did see a flash of light reflect off something they appeared to be holding.

He decided it was time to head on back to town, but as he walked to the Cruiser, he could hear a droning noise in the distance. Holding the binoculars back up to his eyes, he could see something coming his way from the south, probably that same dark spot he'd seen earlier over Horse Bench.

As he watched it come closer, he could tell it had an odd shape, and he knew it was the same aircraft Sammy had spotted. The closer it came the more unsettled Bud began to feel, and once he could clearly make it out, he knew it was unlike anything he'd ever seen before.

It looked like a large egg with three chicken legs attached, with plates on the narrow bottoms of the legs, which Bud assumed were for holding it up in soft sand. He at first thought it might be some strange kind of drone, but as it came closer, he could see two heads looking out a big window in the egg.

His instincts were to jump in the Cruiser and hightail it out of there, but he was too late, for the craft was now directly above him, and the sound was so loud he had to cover his ears. It hovered for a moment, then took off across the river and on in the direction of the small town of Radium.

Senses now recovered, Bud grabbed his camera and began taking photos, glad he'd left his telephoto lens on. The craft receded in the distance, and still in somewhat of a haze, Bud next aimed the lens down toward the river and snapped a few shots of the dories and tiny figures, then got into the Cruiser and headed for town.

Even though it was one of the stranger things he'd ever seen, Bud knew there had to be a logical explanation for the craft. One thing he did know was that its odd shape—the egg, chicken legs, and plates— had made him even hungrier.

He'd give his good friend Sheriff Hum Stocks down in Radium a heads-up, then head on over to the Melon Rind Cafe, then call Sammy to see what they could come up with.

2

Driving along, Bud started humming a tune he hadn't thought of for years, C.W. McCall's *Convoy*. He wasn't sure of the words, but remembered it as having something to do with truckers ganging up and steamrolling state troopers, which they called "smokey bears," and talking to each other on CB radios, saying things like, "That's a 10-4, good buddy."

Smiling, he thought of how his once-deputy, Howie McPherson, had used the same phrase when he'd first started on the force, and Bud had told him it probably wasn't necessary to add the *good buddy* part when on the police radio.

Bud smiled, thinking of how green Howie had been behind the ears when he'd hired him and yet how he'd eventually become sheriff when Bud had quit to farm melons. Howie had occasionally deputized Bud when he needed help, and now Bud was again sheriff, for the county had asked him to come back when Howie was elected Mayor of Green River.

It was an interesting turn of events, kind of like how the truckers had adopted the *10-4* from the smokey bears, who were basically the truckers' sworn enemies when it came to trying to outsmart them.

Bud was about to give up on remembering the song's lyrics—

something about a trucker called Rubber Duck with a huge convoy behind him crashing through a toll gate to avoid paying the toll— when he noticed a distant figure walking along the road ahead.

He was still a good four miles from town, and he wondered who would be out walking this desolate road. Maybe it was some adventure seeker who'd run out of gas or broken down, though he hadn't seen a vehicle.

He slowed as he came alongside the person, and could now see it was a young man dressed in what looked to be near-rags that seemed to be made of gray wool. The man turned, and Bud could see he was a pleasant-looking young fellow with reddish-blonde hair, clutching something that looked like a leather-bound book to his side.

"You need a ride into town?" Bud asked.

"I would be most appreciative, sir," the man replied, getting into the passenger side while asking Bud, "Hoo are ye?"

"I'm Sheriff Bud Shumway, and you?"

"Nay, nay, I mean whit like are ye? Hoo's it goin'?"

The young man grinned, then continued, "Ma name's Andrew, but everyone calls me Andy. See, when I wanna know yer name, I say, 'Whit dae they cry ye?' not 'Hoo are ye?' Hoo's askin' how, not who."

Bud was thoroughly confused. Andy seemed to be quite capable of speaking normally, yet randomly slipped in and out of what appeared to be a Scottish accent, or so Bud guessed.

"I'm fine," Bud replied. "Your car broke down?"

Andy grimaced, then replied, "Car? I dinnae understand."

"Do you speak English?" Bud asked. "I mean, not Scots-English, but regular English."

"Aye, a wee bit."

"Well, you know what a car is. You're in one."

"Aye, but that's after me time, sir."

"Do you mind if I ask where you're from?"

"Whaur? I was born in Roxburghshire, Scotland, in 1848."

Bud was taken back. "1848? Don't you mean 1948? You look too young even for that."

"Eighteen forty eight, and I'm the youngest on the expedition.

Shot and killed guarding a mule train packing a $5,000 mine payroll to Globe, Arizona. I was laid to rest on August 21, 1882. Of course, I won't know all that until after I'm dead. But mate, can you take me to the nearest grocery? I need to resupply."

Now the young man sounded like an Aussie, Bud mused, wondering if he'd somehow picked up a ghost—or maybe a madman.

"I have some clothes about your size if you want them," Bud offered.

"Nae, I'd be considered a traitor. I'd get shot if I went back in regular clothes. Someone's gonna get shot before it's all over and done, but it aren't gonna be me, mate. I already been shot once, ya know, guarding that dang payroll to Globe, and once is enough."

Now thinking he sounded like a Scotts Aussie, Bud asked, "Where are you going back to?"

"The river. Not that I want to go back. There's been strange things happening down there, things not in Dellenbaugh or the Major's books. Screechin' an strange caterwailin', even worse than what's goin' on in our camp. And that pair talkin' about gettin' rid of the oboe player, that was beyond the pale."

Bud was now thoroughly confused, but he knew he'd be even more confused if he asked Andy to explain. As Bud pulled up in front of the Melon Harvest Grocery, Andy opened the door, saying, "Thank ye for the ride, Sheriff. First time I've ever ridden in the front of a sheriff's vehicle—they always put me in the back. Hae a good day."

Before Bud could say anything, Andy had slipped out and was gone into the grocery store, leaving a strong scent of campfire smoke and mustiness in his wake.

Later, after Bud had gone home and was enjoying the evening cool in a white wicker chair on the back patio, his three dogs at his feet, he reflected on all this, as well as on the phone call he'd just had from Sammy, the airport manager. Bud had intended to call him and tell him he'd seen the weird craft, but Sammy had beat him to it.

It seems that Sammy had given this same Andy fellow a ride back from town to the river, dropping him off near the willows, where a small wooden dory was beached.

He was carrying a half-dozen bags of groceries, and when Sammy casually asked what he'd bought, he'd muttered something about how he was sick of wormy bacon and so had bought lots of fresh bacon and flour and yeast, along with a dozen bags of peppermint Life Savers.

Sammy had found the whole thing odd, especially Andy's ragged woolen clothes and his somewhat erratic Scottish accent. As he let Andy out, he could see more dories on the other side of the river with men standing around appearing to be watching for him.

Sammy had advised, "As sheriff, Bud, you might want to look into things out there."

"Were they doing something illegal?" Bud asked, not very eager to look into anything right then, except the possibility of getting another slice of Wilma Jean's apple pie.

"I don't know," Sammy had replied. "But they sure acted suspicious. And that Andy guy, he doesn't look a day over 18, if that. He said something that didn't sound good."

"Oh?" Bud asked.

"Yeah, he said the previous evening while he was hiding behind some tamarisk writing in his journal—it's supposed to be a secret, but he carries it around with him—he said he heard someone say they were going to take care of that dang oboe player."

"He mentioned that oboe player to me, too, but it makes no sense."

"I know. He said it was someone walking along the riverbank. There were two of them, but they disappeared back into the tammies. He couldn't really make them out and he sure wasn't going to go looking for them to ask what they were talking about."

"Understandable," Bud said, now tapping absent-mindedly on the wicker side table as his little dachshund, Pierre, started chewing on his pant leg.

"Add that weird flying egg into the mix and it makes for a strange brew," Sammy added.

Bud replied, "An egg brew—sounds kind of disgusting, though I guess that's what eggnog is."

"I'm not sure what you're talking about, Bud, but I gotta go get some dinner. Just be careful. 10-4, good buddy."

Hanging up and putting his phone in his pocket, Bud wondered why Andy would mention to both him and Sammy, complete strangers, what he'd heard about someone plotting to get rid of an oboe player. It seemed strange, along with everything else about him.

Bud now stood to go get another piece of pie, nearly stepping on Pierre, who was still chewing on his pant leg. Pierre quickly let go and followed Bud in line behind the other dogs, the trio looking like a short-legged little convoy.

3

Bud stood in the candy isle of the Melon Harvest Grocery and Deli, absentmindedly trying to remember what he was looking for, as he seldom bought candy, preferring vanilla-bean ice cream when he wanted something sweet, though he mostly just put a dollop in his coffee.

Trying to remember, he looked over the contents of his cart—several boxes of Barkie Biscuits for the dogs, a head of iceberg lettuce, some carrots, broccoli, red peppers, milk, butter, pancake mix, and a copy of *Lost Treasure Magazine* for Howie.

Bud had been surprised to see the magazine on the stand, as it had gone out of circulation years ago, but apparently someone had started it back up again, which he knew would make Howie happy. He could now retire all those worn-out old copies in his office from the library free box.

The store proprietor, Sherwyn, saw him and stopped.

"Can I help you find something, Bud?"

"I can't for the life of me remember what I wanted to get here, Sher," Bud replied. "If it was something my wife wanted, I'd better just stand here until I remember it. Sorry to block the isle."

"It's OK," Sherwyn replied. "Nobody else in here anyway. But what would your wife want from the candy isle? You guys never buy candy."

Bud smiled. Some things about living in a small town like Green River were good, some not so good. The grocery proprietor knowing your eating habits could fall into either category, depending on if he was ordering stuff you liked or ratting you out to your wife for buying something you shouldn't.

Now tapping on the cart handle, Bud replied, "I think I remember what it was. You know, I have a bad habit I'm trying to break, which is always fiddling with something—it helps me think. Before I met Wilma Jean, I smoked, or maybe fiddled with my cigarette was a better description. But everything I find to replace smoking irritates my wife. So I was thinking maybe if I could find some kind of hard candy—like Life Savers—and maybe if I tried that, my wife wouldn't get so irritated with me. So, I guess I need some Life Savers."

"Hate to tell you, Bud, but that's probably not something the dentist would recommend."

"I know, but I wouldn't have to eat them all the time, just when I needed to think."

"How often do you need to think?" Sherwyn asked. "If you're like most people, you're on automatic pilot and wouldn't go through a bag very often, unless you just craved the sugar."

Bud laughed. "Well, point me to them. I'm gonna give it a shot."

"Better get several bags in case you have some crime you need to solve," Sherwyn laughed, showing Bud to the Life Savers. "But I only sell peppermint, and I only have one bag left. Some guy almost wiped me out. I used to carry wintergreen too, but the kids were buying it to make it spark, and I worried about them eating too much of it, which can make you sick. If you needed to do some deep thinking, you might not want to be eating wintergreen."

Bud asked, "What do you mean they were making it spark?"

Sherwyn replied, "I like to take good care of my customers, especially the kids, so I researched it. When you bite into the wintergreen, you get a tiny spark. It takes two ingredients to make the spark—crystallized sugar and methyl salicylate, or mint flavoring."

"How does that work?" Bud asked.

"Well, when you bite into the sugar crystal, you're tearing the chemical bonds, which creates fragments that are positively and negatively charged. Actually, Bud, it gets complicated..."

"No, I'm interested. Tell me more."

"OK. Biting anything can cause tiny sparks to hop around, which, in turn, excites nitrogen molecules in the air. This creates ultraviolet light, but usually not enough to see. But the methyl salicylate in wintergreen absorbs the ultraviolet light, then re-emits it, increasing the effect, making it so you can see the sparks. It's called triboluminescence, the creation of light by friction. But methyl salicylate can cause respiratory problems and even be toxic if you eat enough."

"How did you figure all that out, Sher? Sounds pretty complicated. But is the peppermint flavor OK?"

"Well, Bud, not many people know this about me, and I'd prefer they didn't, as I'd start getting all kinds of questions about this and that, but I have a degree in chemistry. Peppermint is OK, just don't eat too much of it. Why not start out with one bag and see how it works out, see if it affects your ability to think or not, especially since I only have one bag left."

"Thanks, but just one question—how did you come to major in chemistry?"

Sherwyn groaned. "See, Bud, that's why I don't mention it to anyone. They always ask that same question."

"I don't mean to intrude, Sher, you know that. No need to explain."

"Well, you're OK, Bud, I can tell you because you won't blab it around. But my grandpa was one of those guys who the revenuers were always trying to catch during Prohibition, a moonshiner. They knew he had an illegal still, but they never could catch him."

"Wasn't he over in the Morman Tanks area of the Swell?" Bud asked. "Sher, everyone knows your grandpa was a moonshiner."

Sherwyn answered, "Really? I didn't know that." He paused for a moment, thinking, then continued. "My dad followed in his footsteps, except he was legal, though the funds he used weren't so much, coming from my grandpa. But Dad started a whisky distillery up in Driggs, Idaho and said he'd pay my way through college if I'd major in chemistry and then go to work for him. He wanted to make the best whisky in the world."

"But you opened a grocery store instead?" Bud asked.

"I did, but only after his distillery caught fire and exploded. He had a vapor leak. Fortunately no one was hurt, but that was the end of that."

Sherwyn dropped the last bag of peppermint Life Savers into Bud's cart, then followed him up front to check him out. Bud thanked him, still having a nagging feeling he was forgetting something.

Now on his way home, his phone rang, and he could see from the caller ID that it was Howie, his former deputy.

"Yell-ow," Bud answered.

"Sheriff, where are you?" Howie asked.

"I'm about home, Howie. Something wrong?"

"Things aren't going so good right now, Sheriff," Howie moaned.

Bud waited patiently for Howie to continue, knowing he sometimes had to untangle his emotions from the facts in order to express himself. He could hear what sounded like road noise in the background.

Finally, Howie asked, "You still there, Sheriff?"

"I am," Bud replied, pulling into his driveway.

"Well, my battery gauge is deader than a doorknob," Howie said. "What do you think is going on?"

"Sounds like your alternator. Better pull over while you still have some power."

"Now all the gauges are jumping around like they're possessed— can engines be possessed, Sheriff?" Howie asked excitedly.

"Pull over, Howie," Bud advised. "Where are you?"

"Hang on."

Bud waited, now carrying the groceries into the kitchen. He gave each of the dogs a Barkie Biscuit, then began unloading everything.

Finally, Howie said, "Sheriff, that was downright scary. Everything started jerking and jumping and I was barely able to get off the road.

A big semi was passing me at the same time, and I almost ran into him. Man."

"You OK now?"

"Yeah, except I'm dead in the water. No power, and now everything's deader than a doorknob, not just the battery gauge."

"You mean deader than a doornail. Where are you?"

"I don't even know what a doornail is, Bud. How can it be deader than something I don't even know exists? In any case, it's entirely, unquestionably dead."

"Howie, a dead doornail is one that's been pounded down so it can't be removed and reused. It's an old expression, but nobody knows what a dead doornail is now because nails are too cheap to need to be reused these days. But where are you?"

"I'm sitting by the road just about a mile on the Green River side of Woodside. That's real interesting, Sheriff, but I actually have a bigger problem in that I'm about to get run over. Then I'll be deader than both a doorknob and a doornail."

"Well, hang tight, Howie. I'll come out with a tow strap and pull you into town."

"You can't do that, Sheriff. I'm in an RV. I'm gonna have to call a tow truck."

Bud, now reaching for the freezer handle to put the vanilla-bean ice cream away, realized that was what he'd forgotten. He tried not to groan.

"An RV? You have an RV? OK, I'll be right out with some charging cables. I can get you going for a few miles at a time. We'll limp it home that way. I need to stop by the grocery store on my way back anyway."

"OK, Sheriff. Thanks and 10-4. Try to hurry."

4

Bud sat on the porch swing at Howie's big farm house, Bodie the Maine Coon cat in his lap, holding on tenuously as Bud went higher and higher. Howie sat nearby in an old worn-out recliner, another Maine Coon cat named Tobie in his lap curiously watching Bodie while Howie leafed through the new copy of *Lost Treasure Magazine*.

"This cat has a sense of adventure," Bud noted, swinging even higher. "He's not a bit afraid. He's an adventure cat."

"Yeah, but you should see him when we turn on the vacuum. He'd climb the walls if that's what it took to get away. By the way, Sheriff, thanks for the rescue."

Howie nodded toward a dated white pickup with a large cabover camper parked in front of the house.

"It really didn't take that many charges to get it back," Bud replied. "Are you going to put in a new alternator yourself, Howie? And hows come you guys bought it? I thought you didn't enjoy camping."

"I'll limp it down to the shop. And I *don't* like camping. Saying that makes me feel inadequate, to be honest, as guys are supposed to like camping, but I like having a hot shower every morning. Maureen's the one who wanted it. She loves camping and wants little

Malcolm to get an early start on it. I figure when he's old enough, she'll dump me for him as a camping buddy, which is OK by me."

Bud laughed, thinking of his own uncomfortable camping forays in a tent. Maybe he should consider an RV, he mused, as he wasn't getting any younger.

Howie continued. "She talked me into it by saying we could use it for when the band plays out of town, which is actually pretty rare, but she also said we might need it for mayoral events and such, now that I'm mayor."

"Mayoral events?" Bud asked as Bodie jumped from his lap, sailing into a nearby bush.

"Yeah, things like ribbon cuttings."

"Why would you need an RV for ribbon cuttings when you live within a mile or less of everything in Green River?"

Howie sighed as Tobie jumped down and followed Bodie to the barn.

"Well, see, Sheriff, she read about the mayor of Radium, Mayor Stocks. He's Sheriff Hum's relation, you know, though I'm not sure exactly how. They opened a new swimming pool there and after Mayor Stocks officiated and cut the ribbon, all dressed in a suit, tie, and dress shoes, he jumped into the pool. Everybody thought it was great. I want to keep my constituents happy, like he did."

"I don't know of anyone putting in a pool around here, do you?"

"Wanda Simpson said she and Jim are thinking about buying the old Sweet Dreams Motel, and she told my wife she was tired of traveling with her dogs and never finding a place to stay, so she's going to make it dog-friendly and call it the Bark Park Motel or something like that, complete with a pool shaped like a fire hydrant. If I have to jump into the pool after cutting the ribbon, I'll have the RV right there and can just change on the spot. That's what Maureen said, anyway."

"Howie, Wanda's pretty famous for having wild ideas that never go anywhere. She thinks things up while on her postal rounds. I personally wouldn't worry about it too much."

"She sounded pretty serious—well, at least Maureen said she did."

"You don't think your wife was trying to persuade you, do you?" Bud asked.

"She probably was," Howie replied. "But it's OK, it didn't cost much. It was from the estate of some old guy up in Price, and I got it pretty cheap."

"How many miles?"

"Around 200,000, but it's got a good engine, Sheriff. A Chevy 2400 with a 7.4 liter V8."

Bud nodded approvingly just as his phone rang.

"Yell-ow," he answered.

Howie listened to Bud's end of the conversation, which consisted primarily of uh-huhs, reallys, and hmms. Finally, Bud said, "Thanks for the information. I'll pass it on to Sheriff Stocks, as that's his jurisdiction."

Hanging up, Bud said, "That was Marty, the guide down at Green River Waterways. He was coming up the river in his motor boat when he heard some shooting. Seems some fellas are down there poaching geese. He stopped and talked to them, and he said it was the weirdest bunch he's ever encountered. I'm wondering if Andy wasn't one of them."

"Who's Andy, and exactly why were they weird?" Howie asked.

Bud replied, "I met this guy named Andy on the River Road the other day and gave him a ride into town. Marty said they definitely didn't have licenses, because he asked. He said they told him they'd never heard of such a thing. And they were so curious about his motor boat, asking all kinds of really basic questions like they'd never seen one that he finally left, feeling like they might steal it or something. He said they were a rough-looking bunch and had wooden dories, which he wanted to ask about, but he took off when they started examining his boat. He said one had half his arm missing, and they called him Major."

"Did someone talk his arm off? Was it the upper part or the lower?" Howie quickly added, "OK, I know that's not funny, poor fella. But Bud, did you know this issue of *Lost Treasure* has tests of various metal detectors? Mine's number three in the lineup. That's not bad."

Bud continued. "Marty also said he passed a raft that was going downriver and had six guys in it. They had a bunch of hard cases stacked on the end of the raft with bungee cords holding them on. One was really big and weird-shaped."

"That's an odd way to describe someone, Bud. Not very nice, really."

"No, he was talking about one of the cases, not the rafters. What could it be?"

"Maybe they're looking for placer gold and had a small sluice box," Howie said, continuing to leaf through his magazine. "Or maybe they're musicians who carry a tuba along."

Bud laughed. "Not very likely. But I need to get back to the office. I need to talk to Hum and then do some paperwork."

As Bud stood to go, Howie's phone rang.

"Mayor McPherson here."

After a moment, he signaled for Bud to wait, his eyes big. Bud sat back down, pulling a couple of Life Savers from his pocket and handing one to Howie.

"You're communications and public relations director? That sounds like a very impressive job."

He paused for moment, then said, "No, no, I meant that in a good way, Ms. Chambers, and yes, I know the difference between a symphony and a philharmonic orchestra. Everyone knows that."

Howie was quiet for awhile, listening, then said, "Riccardo Muti? No kidding?"

More silence, then, "Yes, I'm sure you produce spectacular, world-class music."

Then, "Seriously? Of course you're more than welcome. And yes, I know who Stravinsky was, as well as Beethoven. Sir Georg Solti won thirty-one Grammy Awards? Wow!"

And finally, "OK, I'll be waiting for more information, and you know we'll be giving you the key to the city, even though it's not really a city, more of a town, though a pretty small one—some might call it a village, though some might say a hamlet, but it's definitely bigger than a whistle-stop. I'll have to find the key first, though."

Howie hung up, and Bud could see he was starting to hyperventilate a little.

"What's going on, Howie?" He asked, rolling the Life Saver around in his mouth.

"That was this gal from the Chicago Symphony, Sheriff. They're coming to perform in Green River. Where would I find the key to the city? And who's Riccardo Muti? And Sir Georg Solti?"

"Are you sure it wasn't some kind of prank?" Bud asked.

"You think maybe I just got pranked? Oh man..."

Bud asked, "Why would the Chicago Symphony come here? We don't even have a place for them to play. The old flagstone square-dance stage in the park wouldn't even begin to hold an orchestra, and that's the only place we have."

"I should've known it was a prank when she asked if I knew who Beethoven was. Everyone knows who Beethoven was. I'm so gullible," Howie moaned. "Some mayor I am, easily pranked."

"Howie, heads of state have been pranked. But maybe it was real. What else did she say? Are you familiar with the symphony?"

"No, I've actually never even heard of the Chicago Symphony. She said the symphony was famous for their out-of-the-box programming."

"Well, Green River's certainly out of the box," Bud replied. "When are they coming?"

"Bud, this was odd. She said they were already here. That doesn't make any sense. If an orchestra had hit Green River, surely someone would notice. How many people are in an orchestra, anyway?"

"I don't know. Maybe eighty, maybe a hundred."

"An audience here would be smaller than the orchestra—do you know anyone around here who listens to classical? That orchestra's one-eighth of the population of town. Somebody would be sure to notice. Where could we possibly house that many people?"

"We could start with your RV. That's probably good for a couple, then take it from there. Trombone players are usually pretty free-spirited, they might like camping in it, though they'd have to go outside to practice."

"Do you suppose they expect us to house them for free? Man, Sheriff, I'm not liking this one bit. Do you think being mayor is going to be like this all the time?"

"Maybe," Bud grinned. "But Howie, I'm sure they've run into these kind of logistical problems before and wouldn't consider it if they couldn't pull it off, assuming it's for real. And if they're already here, one of us is soon to know, being sheriff and mayor. But I gotta run. Hang in there, good buddy."

"I hope they don't schedule a concert when we have our Rockabilly Night," Howie replied as Bud headed out to his vehicle, then added, "But what *is* the difference between a symphony and a philharmonic orchestra?"

Bud shrugged his shoulders as Howie said, "Speaking of Stravinsky, did you know that his *Rite of Spring* caused a riot at its premiere in France? It was too radical for them. Who ever heard of someone rioting over a piece of classical music? Anyway, 10-4, Sheriff."

5

Bud had just finished lunch at Howie's Drive-In and was heading back to his office, thinking of how it had now been several days and he still hadn't seen any evidence of an orchestra in town.

He was beginning to wonder if maybe Howie hadn't been pranked after all, though he had no idea who would have done it. But he knew that having a visible position like mayor made one open to all kinds of creative possibilities, which he himself had been subjected to as sheriff.

One example he thought was especially odd was when he got a call late one night saying they needed help because they'd checked into a strange hotel. When Bud asked what the problem was, they'd told him it was made up entirely of all the thirteenth floors missing from other hotels. They'd then hung up, laughing. He'd never really understood the point of that one, other than to entertain themselves.

Now near the city park, he saw Howie sitting on a bench in front of the old flagstone square-dance stage with someone who looked to be Eldon Daddage. Bud pulled over and got out, wanting to see if Howie had any more news about the orchestra.

"Howdy, Sheriff," Eldon greeted him. "Did you come to join the wake?"

"Did someone die?" Bud asked. "I don't see a body."

"My good pal Frosty Merriott is about to pass away," Eldon replied. "At least from *my* life, anyway."

Howie shook his head, saying, "Eldon, he'll come around, just give him time."

"He might as well be dead," Eldon mourned. "Our days of hanging around with the Bucket of Bolts Overlanders are over."

"What happened to Frosty?" Bud asked with concern.

Howie, looking irritated, replied, "Nothing. It's just that he and Mrs. Jensen set a date for their wedding, and Eldon can't handle it."

"I can't hang out with a married man," Eldon said. "I have too much integrity. He's no longer a free being. Do this, do that, be home by dinnertime, eat your peas. Frosty and I used to go wherever we wanted, anytime we wanted. The good old days are over. The good old days, that's what the wake's for, not Frosty, though he might as well be dead, too."

"When's the wedding?" Bud asked.

"In two weeks," Eldon replied. "Frosty wants me to be his best man, but I wouldn't be caught dead in a tux. Even if I would be caught dead in one, there's no place to get one except by going clear up to Price."

"Where are they getting married?" Bud asked.

"Right here in the park, right on that stage you're looking at," Eldon replied. "I want to remember it as I knew it from my child-hood, those happy days, people square dancing to the caller—*do si do, roll away to a half sashay*—not as the place for the death of Frosty's freedom."

"You're just enjoying the drama, Eldon," Howie said.

"Now join hands and circle to the south, get a little moonshine in your mouth," Eldon chanted, then added, "Swing 'em high, swing 'em low, turn 'em loose, and watch 'em go."

They all laughed, and seeing his chance to change the subject, Bud asked, "Any news about the missing orchestra, Howie?"

"Still missing," Howie replied desultorily. "Nary even a trio. But say, you have any of those Life Savers on you?"

Bud took several from his pocket and handed them to Howie and Eldon.

"There's a missing orchestra?" Eldon asked, unwrapping the candy. "I need to get on board with the news a little better. What, did someone who hates Ferde Grofé kidnap them or something?" He laughed at his own joke.

"Who's that?" Howie asked.

"The guy who composed the *Grand Canyon Suite*. My ex-wife used to play it all the time. It has this one movement called *On the Trail* that depicts the burros that carry tourists down the canyon, and the music mimics their braying—hee haw, hee haw—the burros, not the tourists. I used to like it, but after about 500 times, I couldn't take it anymore. I made sure it was the first thing she packed when she left. That's what happens when you marry a woman only for love, as in love for her cooking."

Eldon laughed again, then added, "But I gotta go find Junkyard Goldie and see if he has a hubcap for my Jeep. Lost one the other day out in Tusher Canyon."

As they watched Eldon walk to his old Jeep, Howie said, "You never know what trivia some people have in their brains, do you, Sheriff? I would've never guessed Eldon knew anything about classical music."

"Agreed," Bud replied, then added, "Busy day, eh Mayor?"

"Actually, I *am* working, Sheriff," Howie replied with irritation. "Being mayor isn't a full-time job anyway, you know that. But I'm trying to figure out how to enlarge the bandstand here to fit an orchestra."

"If the orchestra's already here, you're running out of time," Bud said, unwrapping another Life Saver.

Howie held out his hand, saying, "Man, those things are addictive."

As Bud handed Howie a couple more candies, his phone rang, and he could see from the caller ID that it was Sheriff Stocks down in Radium.

"Yell-ow," Bud answered.

"Bud, Hum here. I have some news you're not gonna like."

"Go ahead, Hum."

"Well, since the river's the line between our counties, you know we get calls from people recreating in your area, thinking that just because Radium's closer, they're in our jurisdiction. Well, we got a situation going on that really *is* your deal, and I need you to get involved."

"What's going on, Hum?" Bud asked, feeling his stomach tighten. Usually, Hum covered such cases anyway unless they were something major, like a lost hiker or such, then he would usually just call the Radium Search and Rescue, though sometimes the Emery County SAR would also get involved. Hum seldom called on Bud to get involved in a situation, so he knew it had to be something he probably was going to wish he didn't have to deal with.

"Somebody lost?" Bud asked hopefully, knowing he could just get the Emery County SAR involved.

Howie now perked up, listening.

"Worse than that, Bud. You know I hate this job when we have to deal with this kind of thing, but we just got a call from a hiker who found a body. We have the GPS coordinates, and the guy's waiting for us. It's actually on your side of the river, but I've called in Tim Wells' chopper to go out there, as it's too far by road. I need you to check it out. Tim's going to pick you up in about 20 minutes, just enough time for you to get out to the airport. It's out by Spanish Bottom."

"Hum, that's in Wayne County. Shouldn't you call them?"

"The roads in there are in Emery County for the most part," Hum replied unconvincingly.

Bud replied, "Since when do roads in count? If you use that criterion, I could be responsible for Salt Lake City, since the roads here eventually go there."

Hum sounded frustrated. "Bud, Wayne County wants you to cover it, and so do I. They're not as familiar with the area as you are, and you know all the rangers out there, not to mention the country. Plus they're short-handed. We'll all owe you one. And Tim's probably at the airport by now."

"Roger," Bud replied, resigned. "I'm on my way."

"Cal's going along. He's with Tim. He can fill you in on the details, though we really don't have much yet, and we want you to do the report. We're swamped right now. We've been getting calls the past few days from various rafters coming off the river at Mineral Bottom saying they were harassed by some boaters down on the Green. Cal can tell you more. I don't know if it's related or not."

"Any idea who the deceased is?" Bud asked.

"No idea at all."

"Does it look like foul play was involved?"

"No idea at this point, Bud. This hiker just came upon a body and had a cell signal, so he called it in. I told him to stand by and not get near it, as he might mess up any evidence. He's pretty shook up and wants a ride out at this point, so Tim's going to take him back out with you and Cal."

"Roger," Bud replied.

"One last thing, Bud. This is really odd, but the deceased is wearing a tuxedo."

"A tux?" Bud asked, thinking of what Eldon had just said about how he wouldn't be caught dead in a tux. It looked like there was some guy out there who felt differently.

He then asked, "Exactly where is he?"

"In the Maze, Bud. Not far from the river, by the Dollhouse."

"What in hellsbells is a guy wearing a tux doing in the Maze?" He asked.

"That's what you need to figure out, Sheriff," Hum replied.

"But Hum, that's in Canyonlands National Park. That's their jurisdiction. It looks like everyone's passing the buck here. Why aren't they covering it?"

"They're too busy with a visiting dignitary. I talked to them, and they asked us to cover it, at least for now. I owe them a big favor anyway for when they helped out with a bunch of people stuck on the wrong side of a flashflood. But I gotta go."

"Roger," Bud said, the knot in his stomach getting tighter. "10-4."

Bud was soon in the Land Cruiser and on his way to the airport, his emergency pack by his side. He'd thought about stopping by the Melon Rind Cafe to grab a bite to go, but knowing Tim Wells, he knew he wouldn't have time, for Tim wouldn't tarry.

Checking his shirt pocket, he was glad he'd filled it with Life Savers that morning. He sighed, wishing he was instead on his way out to the farm to play ball with the dogs, but he knew that if Tim and Cal were involved, they were two of the most competent people around, and everything would be alright.

What he didn't know was how long it would take for everything to return to being alright.

6

"Another fine day ruined by financial responsibility," Cal said, sitting in the seat behind Bud as Tim prepared to take off from the Green River Airport.

"I take it you don't like this part of your job," Bud replied.

"It's OK when we're not flying in to retrieve a body," Cal replied. "But I will say that after I retire, I'm never getting into another aircraft of any kind."

"No flying to the Bahamas or Hawaii or that kind of thing?" Tim asked, grinning.

"Nope," Cal replied.

"How long before you retire?" Bud asked.

"I don't wanna think about it," Cal muttered, turning his gaze out the window.

Bud had offered for Cal to ride in the front of the chopper, but he'd declined, saying he liked a little something more than thin air under his feet.

Now, after Tim had them test their headsets, Bud turned to look out the window of the older Bell 206. Tim had told them he'd bought it for a song, made some repairs, and it was now painted a bright red, with the words, "Redrock Rover," on the side.

Bud knew that Radium County contracted with Tim for all kinds of things requiring a chopper, from search and rescue to flying equipment around, and Tim would give free rides to people going to Salt Lake for medical treatments. He'd even taken a dog up there once for cataract surgery.

As the helicopter lifted off, Bud could see the small stand of tamarisk around the tiny cold-water geyser by the airport, then he could make out the broken pavement of the old highway to Hanksville. They were soon above the confluence of the Green and San Rafael rivers.

Even though his wife owned a plane and was a pilot, Bud didn't take to the air often, as it made him queasy. He couldn't relax, and he worried the entire time he was up, so he generally avoided it.

Reaching into his pocket, he took out several Life Savers, handing Tim and Cal each a couple, then popped one into his mouth, rolling it around.

They rode along without talking, and Bud knew they were all as intrigued with the rugged and wild landscape beneath them as he was, especially when it came to the Green River and its deep canyons. Its beauty could be spellbinding, in spite of its sometimes harshness.

Now Tim began following the Green, and it wasn't long before they were at the confluence of it and the Colorado, where the clear waters of the Green drifted down some distance before merging with the muddy waters of the Colorado, making the river look like striped toothpaste. Must've been some heavy rains on up higher, Bud thought, making the waters the reddish color the Colorado was named for.

They continued on, and even though Tim was keeping the chopper at a fairly low altitude, Bud could still make out a labyrinth of deep canyons to his right, twisting and turning onto each other like snakes biting their own tails, each canyon looking exactly like the next. He knew he was looking into the Maze, some of the most inhospitable country in North America, and Bud wondered what a fellow dressed in a tuxedo would be doing out there. Something not very good for his health, he mused, hoping they could quickly take care of business and get back home.

Tim veered away from the river above a cleft in the cliffs that led into a tilted valley that Bud knew was called Surprise Valley, a surprise because it existed where a valley shouldn't. It was a graben, the result of salts collapsing far below. They then flew across an arroyo that wound along until it fell off the steep cliffs into the river far below.

Bud could now see the collection of variegated rust and white spires and hoodoos in the area called the Dollhouse, named over a hundred years before by cowboys running stock in the area. He knew the strange forms were made of Cedar Mesa Sandstone that had weathered into all kinds of odd shapes and were reached by climbing a steep trail from Spanish Bottom on the river a good thousand or more feet below. One could also come in from the other direction by vehicle if they had good clearance and didn't mind the torturous switchbacks of the Flint Trail and the Golden Stairs.

He'd been down the Flint Trail before with Eldon's Bucket of Bolts Overlanders, or BOB-O's, and understood why the Park Service told travelers that driving it involved considerable risk of vehicle damage. It had taken them hours to drive only a few miles.

Tim was following the GPS on the chopper, which was leading them to a nearby set of large white biscuit-shaped rocks. As they lost elevation, Bud could see a figure waving at them, a backpack at his feet. He knew it had to be the unfortunate hiker who had found the even more unfortunate body.

He expected Tim to land, but instead he veered a little to the left, landing near the base of a group of spires that made up some of the dolls of the Dollhouse.

As he carefully set the chopper down, Tim said over their headsets, "When you guys get out, be sure to duck down low. I'm going to leave this thing running for awhile to try to keep my cycle count low. And it's not long until sunset, so we need to get out before it gets dark."

Bud and Cal exited the chopper just as the hiker came running over, dragging his backpack behind him. He was a tall thin guy maybe in his 30s with long brown hair tied in a pony-tail. Bud thought that he looked like he was about to burst out crying.

"You guys aren't leaving without me," he said, heading for the chopper.

Cal stopped him, saying, "Just hang on there a minute, buddy. We're not going anywhere, and we need you to tell us what happened. You OK? Need some water? Just relax. We're not going to leave you. What are you doing here, anyway?"

"I hiked down from the Hans Flat Ranger Station and planned on spending a week in the Maze until all this happened. Now I can't wait to get out of here. This is the creepiest place I've ever been."

"OK," Cal continued, pointing at some red rocks. "Go over there in the shade for a bit with Sheriff Shumway here while I check things out."

Bud offered the guy a Life Saver, which seemed to help calm him down, then led him over into the shadow of one of the hoodoos as Cal walked over to check on the body.

Soon back, Cal said, "Now then, I'm Deputy Cal Murphy from the Radium County Sheriff's Department, and this here is Sheriff Bud Shumway of Emery County. And who are you?"

Sucking on the Life Saver, the man replied, "I'm Tex O'Casey."

"I take it you're from Texas?" Cal asked.

"Missoula, Montana."

"Why the Tex?"

Bud smiled, knowing that Cal was trying to establish a connection with the young guy to make him feel more comfortable.

"Because I went to college at the University of Texas and picked up the accent, and when I went back home everyone started calling me Tex. It just kind of stuck."

"What did you major in, Tex?" Cal persisted.

"Structural engineering."

Cal whistled. "That sounds like a hard way to make a living. You design buildings and bridges?"

"No, I specialize in aircraft. I worked for Boeing for awhile, but now I'm doing consulting work. But can we get on with things? I feel really uncomfortable here."

"Sure, sure," Cal replied. "Tell us what happened. Can you show the Sheriff here some ID? You don't mind if I record this, do you?"

"Sure, record away," the guy said, digging his driver's license from his shirt and handing it to Bud.

He said, "I was camped here at the Dollhouse last night and really enjoying being out here. I love the desert, even though I haven't spent that much time in it. Since I'm backpacking, I try to travel light and don't carry a tent, just a tarp for rain. So I was lying out here in the sand and looking at the stars when I heard the weirdest sound I've ever heard in my entire life."

He paused, looking at the nearby rocks, then said, "It's hard to describe, but it was like a combination of a crazed insane mountain lion and a mad duck devil. That was followed by someone playing beautiful music, then by some yelling. I wasn't sure what to do, so I got a big stick from a juniper tree and hid in the rocks, waiting."

Bud took a photo of the ID with his pocket camera, then handed it back to Tex, who continued.

"Whatever it was, I realized it was up in the rocks above me, up high."

"Can you describe what it sounded like in more detail?" Bud asked.

"The first sound was penetrating and biting—maybe you would say piercing. It was unholy sounding. Then to be followed by a beautiful song, then yelling—I was afraid to go to sleep, so I sat in the rocks all night. At dawn, I started to head out, deciding I'd go back to the ranger station at Hans Flat and forego the trip. I can tell you, I was pretty freaked out. That's when I found the guy lying dead over there."

He pointed to a shadowy area under a cliff, adding, "I know something unnatural killed him. There's some strange duck-like petroglyphs over there by where he died. Can we leave now? It's going to be dark soon."

"Well, we have to retrieve his body and look around first, Tex. You gonna be OK?" Cal asked.

"I'm fine. Can I go over by the chopper and wait?"

"Actually," Bud suggested, "Why don't you go get in the chopper. I'll walk over with you and introduce you to the pilot, as I need to get a body bag."

Tex grimaced, then replied, "I'm being a big baby. I'll get the bag for you and help you carry the guy out."

Cal said, "That's good of you, Tex, but it's probably best if you just stay over there. No point in being traumatized again."

"I wasn't traumatized that much," Tex replied. "The guy just looks like he's sleeping. It's wondering what killed him that's got me all shook up. I just want to get out of here."

He stood and walked over to the chopper, as Bud and Cal went to where the body lay, looking for signs of tracks or anything unusual. They were soon at the base of the cliff and could see a small wiry man lying on his back in the sand wearing a tuxedo, who, as Tex had said, looked like he was just taking a nap.

"He could've just fallen from the cliff," Cal remarked. "I'm not seeing many signs of foul play here, Bud."

"It's possible," Bud replied. "He wouldn't be the first such fatality here in the canyons."

Bud took photos of everything as he and Cal continued their search, finding nothing unusual. He then placed some small rocks around the body for measurements later, in case he needed to come back, as he knew time was running out.

Bud then searched the man's pockets as Cal went for a body bag. He hated this part of his job, but at least it didn't happen too often, and this guy wasn't too bad to deal with.

He paused for a moment, wondering if the fellow had a family and what his life had been like, and once again, why he would be wearing a black tux out in the desert. Carefully, he pulled a cell phone and two business cards from the guy's front pocket, sticking them into a baggie, then turned him over.

Something long and narrow was underneath him. Bud hesitated, then carefully picked it up, again using a baggie, shaking off the sand.

It was a shiny black oboe with the word *Yamaha* in gold across its base.

7

Bud stood in surprise, recalling what Andy had said about overhearing someone plotting to kill an oboe player. Putting the instrument in the bag, he next examined the business cards he'd taken from the man's pocket.

The first read:

Reece Billings, Principal Oboist, Chicago Symphony Orchestra, 312-294-3345

And the second:

George Picco, Picco Avionics, Chicago Executive Airport, Wheeling, IL 312-494-6700

Bud held his breath for a moment, somehow suspecting the answer to the man's death was held in those two cards, but how, he had no idea.

He sighed, knowing that nothing about this was going to be easy, then helped Cal get the body back to the waiting chopper. They needed to get going, as the shadows were lengthening. He'd have to come back another time to do his measurements.

They loaded the body, then, after Tim had raised the chopper from its resting place, Bud asked, "Tim, could you radio Sammy and have him get an ambulance to meet us? Be sure to tell them it's a fatality."

As Tim nodded an affirmative, Bud continued, "And would it be possible to fly up the Green on our way back? Actually, head down the Colorado for a mile or two first, since we're here. I'm wanting to look for a bunch of dories that were on the river up by town a few days ago."

"That sounds like the same bunch we've been getting reports about, Bud," Cal replied.

"That's what Hum said. What kind of reports?"

"We've had several canoeists call in saying they'd been harassed. Apparently that bunch was asking for food and such to the point that the boaters felt uncomfortable. Maybe demanding would be a better way to put it."

"Sounds like a bunch of pirates," Bud replied as Tim began following the river downstream.

Tim asked, "Bud, the Green River ambulance is out on a car accident. Should I call the one from Radium?"

"That OK with you, Cal?" Bud asked. "You guys want to cover the autopsy and call me when it's done?"

"Doesn't look like we have much choice, unless we want to take this guy to the coroner in the back of a cruiser. Go ahead, Tim."

The sun set on the horizon like a giant red ball, and Bud could see its last rays lighting up the maroon and pink horizontal bands of the Dollhouse, making them glow like fire. Everyone was quiet, studying the amazing scene below.

Soon Bud could make out a small blotch of yellow along Spanish Bottom, and as Tim flew lower, he could see that it was a raft that appeared to be tied to the tammies on a small sandy beach. There was no one around, nor any sign of a camp. Tim circled lower to where Bud could see that the raft was empty.

He could barely make out the words on its side, *Green River Waterways,* before Tim headed back upstream, commenting that it was time to go if they were going to be back before dark.

As they started back up the river, Bud now could see a wooden dory tied off a short distance up the beach from the raft. It looked to Bud like one of those he'd seen when looking through his binoculars. It had been several days since then, but in order for it to be one of the dories, it would've had to have made really good time. Again, there was no one around, so they continued upriver, soon reaching the confluence, where Tim began following the Green upstream.

As Bud gazed out, he thought about the body they'd just recovered, and it finally dawned on him that there was a possibility that this oboe player might have something to do with the call Howie had received from the supposed Chicago Symphony, assuming it actually hadn't been a prank.

Had the orchestra somehow ended up in the Maze instead of in the town of Green River? If so, how would that work? Eighty to a hundred people?

Who would have enough boat power to carry that many people? And even if they could make their way into the Maze, it made no sense. Why go there in the first place?

He shook his head, unwrapping another Life Saver. Handing several to Tim and Cal, he noticed that Tex was fast asleep, his head leaning back against the seat's headrest.

"Circle round and check that camp out," Cal told Tim, pointing to a wide beach below. "It looks like the rascals we've been hearing about."

Bud could see three wooden dories tied up near what appeared to be sleeping bags laid out on the sand, a huge bonfire throwing sparks into the evening air as a group of rough-looking men stood nearby.

"You have good eyes, Cal," Tim remarked, circling the camp, and Bud could see the men now shaking their fists at the chopper, some even tossing rocks their way, though the aircraft was too high to hit. Now several had picked up what appeared to be rifles, pointing them menacingly into the air.

"I'm backing off," Tim said, the chopper gaining altitude.

"That's the bunch, alright," Bud said. "Wild as ever."

"The Wild Bunch," Cal remarked. "I have a mind to arrest them all, except I don't know what we'd do with them."

Bud could see a man who appeared to have only part of an arm, and he knew it must be the one they'd called the Major. He was angrily gesticulating at the men with his good arm, and they'd put down their guns and were now waving for the chopper to land.

"Not likely," Tim said over the headsets. "They look like outlaws or something."

As the chopper gained altitude, Cal said, "If they keep it up, I *will* come down here and arrest them. We can use jet boats. Put 'em all in jail."

"They aren't making very good time down the river," Bud remarked. They were at Crystal Geyser a few days ago."

"That's a good 60 miles, Bud," Cal replied. "The river's low. I'd call that OK time."

Cal now pointed to their left.

"That's Hell Roaring Canyon over there. There's a *D. Julien* signature on the rocks a short distance up from the river there. All his signatures had a sail carved with them, and they think he used a sail to go down the river."

"When was this?" Tim asked.

Cal replied, "1830s. He was a fur trapper born in 1772. One of the first non-natives in the area. He carved several inscriptions down the rivers—even one over in Colorado. His name has been found carved into rock walls as far north as the Uinta Mountains and as far south as lower Cataract Canyon."

"That's one social media account I'd follow," Tim replied. "Hows come you to know the Green so well, especially living in Radium?"

"We used to go on the Friendship Cruises," Cal replied. "Green River to the confluence, then up the Colorado to Radium. Lots of fun, but then my wife got all into horses. Not so much fun, 'cause unlike boats, they take daily maintenance."

Bud, only half-listening, said to himself, "An orchestra *could* disappear in this country, but how would it happen?"

"What's that about an orchestra?" Tim asked.

"Nothing," Bud replied. "Just talking to myself."

"I do that all the time," Cal replied. "Words just appear from nowhere, then I realize it's actually my wife putting ideas into my head, stuff like go mow the lawn."

Bud laughed. Just then, he caught a glimpse of something high above, flashing in the last sunrays. He at first thought it was an airliner, then, realizing it was too low and odd-shaped, asked, "You fellas see that thing shining up there? Is it a weather balloon?"

After studying it for a moment, Cal said, "It looks like that weird thing you called Hum about the other day."

As it disappeared, Tim said, "I've seen it around here before. It's definitely odd looking, but I think it's a gyrocopter. But if it is, it's pushing the envelope. It doesn't look very stable, and I suspect it's a home brew, probably illegal as all get out."

"You don't know who it is?" Bud asked. "Must be someone local, it's around so much."

"Bud, I know virtually everyone in the aircraft biz for a good 1,000 square miles, but I have no idea who that is."

"A thousand square miles is 100 miles squared," Cal said. "That's not a whole lot of distance in aviation, a box 100 miles each side."

"Actually, Cal," Bud said. "A box like that is one-hundred miles squared, which is 100 times 100 or 10,000 square miles, which is bigger than the state of Vermont. But maybe Tim means a box 1,000 miles each side, which is still pretty big."

"Maybe he means a box 1,000 miles tall and one mile wide," Cal joked. "Or hows about 100 miles tall by 10 miles wide. Which is it, Tim?"

Tim replied, "One of you mathematical geniuses needs to wake our new friend Tex up back there. Looks like Sammy remembered to turn on the airport lights."

With that, they were soon on the ground at the Green River Airport, its runway lights flashing like the sunrays hitting the strange aircraft they'd just seen.

8

Bud rolled around in the old office chair in his equipment shed, the cement floor smooth like a racetrack, while the dogs sat by the door looking worried he might run over them.

Stopping to pop a Life Saver into his mouth, Bud realized it was the last one in his pocket and felt a moment of panic. He then remembered that the bag in his old FJ was still about a third full. He'd have to go get a few bags down at the Melon Harvest to make sure his new fiddling technique didn't catch him empty handed, assuming Sherwyn had gotten in a new shipment.

He paused. Maybe Sherwyn was right, and using candy to think wasn't necessarily a good idea after all. He was afraid to look and see how many calories each piece had, but he knew since they were sweet, they had to have some, and his belt had started feeling a little tighter since he'd started this new habit.

He opened the door and let the dogs out, Lindie, a Carolina Dingo, carrying a ball in her mouth, while the dachshund, Pierre, and Basset hound, Hoppie, headed for the ditch, looking perplexed upon finding it dry.

Bud smiled, saying, "Let's go walk the ditches. We need the exercise."

The dogs took off ahead of him, walking and sniffing along the road next to the ditch, Lindie forgetting all about her ball. The fields were barren and cold-looking, Bud's farm manager Kale having plowed everything under for winter. An occasional melon that the harvest had missed lay here and there, turning brown and melting back into the dirt.

It was Bud's least favorite time on the farm. Even though it meant long work days were ahead, he thought maybe he liked spring best, when the big cottonwoods were starting to green up—or maybe it was autumn, when the harvest was done and the trees were a bright gold against a deep blue sky. And winter could also be beautiful with snows turning the fields into long expanses like something from Dr. Zhivago.

But the transition between fall and winter was usually bleak, the migrating buzzards floating in wide circles high above the fields as a portent of what was to come—lots of cold windy days that would carry your optimism away like the winds took the leaves.

Now Bud could see his wife's big pink Mary Kay Lincoln Continental pull up next to his FJ. As he turned to head back, he could see her wave, put something on his dash, then get back in her car and drive away.

Bud grinned, continuing on his walk. He'd told her he had to go out to Temple Mountain that afternoon, and she'd said she would bring him a surprise. He wasn't sure, but hoped it would be something to eat, as he knew it was bake day for the cafe, and it would be a long afternoon driving almost all the way to Hanksville and back.

Now Lindie picked up a long stick and kept tripping Bud with it, wanting him to throw it, so he broke it in half and tossed one half for her, hiding the other behind a tree for a future walk.

He began thinking about the events of the past few days, specifically the dead oboe player and the yellow raft. Was there a connection? Had the oboe player been one of those on the raft he'd seen a few days before? It was cold enough that he'd figured it was a day trip as they'd only had one boat, but had they intended to camp? It was getting too cold, though there were some diehards that still did it this time of year, including the band of pirates with the one-armed leader that Andy seemed to be a part of.

Was the yellow raft empty because the rafters had gone up by the Dollhouse, somewhere near where he and Cal had found the body? And what was the dory doing there? He wished now that he'd had Tim fly around the Dollhouse a bit before they'd left. He then wondered how long it would take to hear back from Cal about the results of the autopsy.

Bud thought about the phone call Howie had received from the supposed representative of the Chicago Symphony. He'd asked Howie later if he'd heard anything new from them and Howie had said no, so Bud had begun to think it was a prank, but maybe it wasn't. Maybe there was some misunderstanding—Howie was certainly excited enough that he might have misheard.

And what about Howie's comment that maybe the rafters were musicians who carried a tuba along? Maybe he was closer to the truth than Bud had given him credit for. Was it possible that only part of the symphony was here, and why would they have hired a Green River Waterways raft to take them down the river?

This brought Bud to the fellows on the wooden dories. What in hellsbells were they doing? Andy had looked and acted half-starved when Bud had given him a ride, and the bunch trying to cajole others to give them food seemed odd.

And why were they in wooden dories in the first place? And wearing woolen clothes, or what was left of them? And why did they act like they were from another century and had never seen a motorboat?

He recalled Andy pretending he didn't know what a car was, as well as his obviously fake Scottish accent and total delight in getting the bags of Life Savers. And why did the guy have only half his arm? What had happened to it? Was he really a Major? Why did that ring a bell, yet he couldn't quite put his finger on what it all meant?

Lindie had now forgotten the stick and was chasing after a squirrel, the boys trying to keep up but too slow. Bud now thought of the call he'd received the previous evening, not long after he'd gotten back from the body recovery.

It was from Carl Chapman, a law-enforcement officer with the BLM, or Bureau of Land Management, down in Radium. The BLM managed millions of acres in Utah, including much of the land in Emery County. Bud had worked with Carl before on cases and knew his office was sorely understaffed.

Carl had asked Bud if he would mind going over to Temple Mountain, which was west of the Maze and in Emery County, to check on a couple of reports they'd gotten about someone opening a business on BLM land over there.

"What kind of a business would one open at Temple Mountain?" Bud had asked incredulously. "The uranium boom days over there are long gone."

"We're getting reports that some gal has a cafe going," Carl had replied. "It's completely illegal to run a business on BLM property, though there are occasional exceptions, but this isn't one of them. I would be most appreciative if you could drive down that way and check it out for me, Bud. I'm so busy down here I hardly have time to sleep these days."

Bud was tempted to make a joke about how Carl should try to sleep at night instead of by day, but he held back, knowing the guy was stressed.

"I'd be glad to help you out, Carl, especially seeing how you've done the same for me. Tomorrow's my day off, and it'll give me a good excuse to get out in the backcountry. But I have something I'd like to recommend for stress—Life Savers. They've really helped me out lately."

"Bud, could you be a little more specific? What kind of life savers?"

Bud laughed. "You know, the little round candy ones. There's something about them that's really soothing—at least the peppermint ones."

Carl was quiet for a minute, then said, "You're not joking with me, are you, Bud? I have heard that peppermint tea is relaxing."

"Probably the same principle, but you can't carry tea around in your pocket. Give it a try. I'll go down tomorrow afternoon and check things out. 10-4."

Bud and the dogs were now back by the equipment shed, where he locked the door. He'd drop the two little dogs off at the bungalow, make a thermos of coffee, then he and Lindie would head on down to Temple Mountain.

He could now see that Wilma Jean had left something wrapped in tinfoil on the dash. As he picked it up, he could tell it was some kind of pie. Taped to it was a note.

Hon, this cherry pie isn't quite done, so leave it on the dash as you drive along. The sun will finish it. It'll be nice and warm when you get there. XXOO

Next to the pie was a small sack containing several paper plates, as well as forks and napkins.

Bud grinned, turned the FJ around, and headed for the bungalow to leave Hoppie and Pierre there, along with a small pile of Barkie Biscuits.

9

Bud hadn't been down the old highway from Green River to Hanksville for several years, so on a last minute whim, he turned and headed for the Airport Road instead of the freeway. Lindie rode shotgun, excited to be going along.

They were soon on old State Highway 24, which veered from the Airport Road and cut across the Mancos clay badlands. It eventually reached Jessie's Twist, an area of curves that cut down through the eroded landscape of the Morrison Formation, coming out near the Hatt Ranch, where it met up with the newer highway to Hanksville.

The old road had been used as a shortcut by the locals ever since it had been abandoned, but it was now so eroded and buckled that Bud wondered if it were even still passable. Every once in awhile he had to slow down to avoid potholes, some which had grown considerably since his last passage over the old road, and shadscale grew between the cracks in the deteriorating asphalt.

He was beginning to think he'd made a mistake in coming this way, as it was easily taking twice as long, yet he was enjoying the remoteness and feeling of solitude he always got when out in what he called the Big Empty.

Negotiating the curves of Jessie's Twist, he finally dropped down to an old bridge crossing a wash, then connected with the highway, now going toward Hanksville. The huge white flatirons of the San Rafael Reef stood to the west, tipped with the deep reds of Entrada Sandstone, as rugged and intimidating as a coral reef would be to a seafarer.

He was now crossing a big red desert that could have easily been lifted from the Rub' al Khali in Saudi Arabia, the red sands drifting across the highway in low spots, a constant irritant to the highway crews.

Bud had seen photos of that big Arabian desert and was amazed at how much it resembled this area, though much larger, stretching across much of the Arabian Peninsula. He was glad he was here and not there, for the landscape here was much more quantifiable, bordered by Mancos and Morrison cliffs to the north, by the San Rafael Reef to the west, and by the Henry Mountains to the south—and to the east by the hopelessly twisty canyons of the Maze.

Bud knew that, like other deserts, the inhabitants here included such characters as scorpions and giant desert centipedes, which fortunately weren't as fond of the Green River area, preferring the sands of the Entrada to the clays of the Mancos. He had seen scorpions near Green River, but they weren't as common as in the red desert here.

Stands of ancient blackbrush were all that seemed to hold the desert together, with long rows of rabbitbrush and fourwing saltbrush lining the arroyos that came from the distant breaks in the Reef, that rampart that protected the huge landmass behind it known as the San Rafael Swell.

The highway was now straight as an arrow, and he made up for the time he'd lost on the old road. Traffic was sparse, and he soon reached an intersection where a sign read, "Goblin Valley State Park." Bud knew that this had once been the site of the Temple Mountain Motel and Gas Station, built in the 1950s to service the many uranium miners that hoped they were on the road to riches with their doghole mines.

Turning, he was now on the Temple Mountain Road, and could

soon see a break in the Reef. Through the opening he saw where the two large cliffs of a white and gray mountain were held together by rubble melting into time. It was 6,820-foot Temple Mountain, named for its obvious similarity to a temple, probably the big Mormon one in Salt Lake City, Bud figured. He knew that at 1,200 feet above its surroundings, it was the highest point along the Reef.

Driving along, another road soon intersected on the left, but he continued forward, not wanting to go to Goblin Valley, a large basin filled with odd-shaped erosional features of Entrada Sandstone that was once called Mushroom Valley by the old-time cowboys.

He'd been there a number of times and enjoyed its whimsical and even threatening-looking hoodoos, and his childhood Boy Scout troop up in Price had even camped there one Halloween night just for fun, scaring the bejeebers out of each other with practical jokes.

Now the road cut through the Reef itself, following a wide wash, and Bud could see someone walking along, who, upon hearing him, turned and stuck out his thumb.

It was Tex! Bud was surprised, as last he'd seen him, he was checking into the Desert Rose Motel in Green River the previous night, so tired Bud figured he'd sleep for a couple of days. He must've gotten up early to hitch down here, Bud mused.

"Need a ride?" He asked, pulling over, telling Lindie to jump in the back.

Tex, looking surprised, put his pack next to Lindie, then, as he got in, remarked, "Thanks for stopping, Sheriff. Something sure smells good."

Bud grinned. "I'm baking a cherry pie," he said, nodding toward the pie on the dash. "You can have some when we stop. Call me Bud. Where you headed?"

"Well, Bud," Tex replied tenuously. "I gave up on the Maze after all that, so I decided I'd come over here and explore. I know there are some really big canyons here, too, and these even have wild burros. I got a ride from Green River with some guys going to hike Wild Horse and Bell. They dropped me off at the Goblin intersection."

Bud nodded, knowing that the two popular slot canyons were on down past Goblin.

He asked, "You going behind the Reef then?"

Tex replied, "I'm not sure. I guess so, since we're almost through it. But there's a cafe up here, so I decided to just head this way. I haven't had a hot meal since...well, this morning's breakfast at the Chow Down. But I know it'll be awhile before I get another."

"Don't you carry food with you?" Bud asked.

"Well, sure. There's nothing to eat out here, unless you're like a raven and eat lizards. I have lots of freeze-dried food, but it's like this, when you've hiked 15 miles, it's a gourmet feast, but if you were to get it in a restaurant, you'd send it back. What are you doing so far from home?"

Bud replied, "Same as you, going to the cafe."

"Are you taking them a pie or something?" Tex asked.

"No, that's for me. My wife made it. I carry pies around with me in case wherever I stop doesn't have dessert."

Lindie now crawled on top of Tex's pack, her head nearly touching the FJ's ceiling. Bud told her to get down, but she ignored him, enjoying the view.

"She's OK," Tex said. "I miss my dog. I left him with my parents in Missoula. It's too hard trying to explore the desert with a dog when you have to carry enough water for the two of you and he's wearing a fur coat. But I sure wished I had him when that weird noise came around in the Maze. That still has me shook up."

Bud nodded in agreement, then said, "Say, Tex, what would you think if I told you it was that guy playing an oboe?"

Tex was quiet for some time, then said, "I guess it makes sense— actually, it makes a lot of sense. An oboe could easily make all the weird sounds I heard. But why would he be playing an oboe?"

"I don't know," Bud replied, now wondering if he'd said too much. He didn't regard Tex as a suspect, but one never knew. "Maybe for the same reason he was wearing a tux."

"Some kind of concert?" Tex asked, puzzled, then continued. "You know, Bud, I never mentioned this other thing that happened out there because I thought I was hallucinating. But first, let me give you a little background to help explain."

He continued. "One time, I had a really creepy hiking experience. I hiked up this mountain in Montana—Trappers Peak, over by Darby, if you know the country—and all the time I could hear muffled voices following me, yet I never saw any people. I'd stop, but the sounds always stayed the same distance behind me. Finally, I took off my pack to get some water, totally freaked out and deciding to head back, when I discovered I'd left my little portable radio turned on, buried deep inside my pack. So that taught me that weird things usually have an explanation."

Bud patiently waited for Tex to continue as they now exited the tight canyon, the country called Behind the Reef opening up.

Tex said, "OK, well, given that, you can see maybe why I didn't mention this to you guys, but the whole time I was out there, I kept hearing music playing in the distance. It was really spooky."

"What kind of music?" Bud asked, the bleached, dirty-white Wingate Sandstone cliffs of Temple Mountain towering in the distance.

"It was classical music, like a chamber orchestra or woodwind quintet or whatever you call it."

"Was an oboe playing?"

"I don't know, it's hard to pick out each instrument at a distance," Tex said thoughtfully. "It sounded like a clarinet, a flute, a bassoon, and horn, and maybe an oboe, but maybe not."

"You know the instruments well enough to recognize each one?"

"I do. My mom's a classical nut. There's a woodwind quintet in Montana called the Chinook Winds, and she used to drag me along to their concerts."

"Without an oboe, it would be a quartet," Bud said.

"Once in awhile I could also hear what sounded like a guitar, but it was usually drowned out by the others."

"A guitar? Odd," Bud said. "But it looks like we're at the cafe."

Pulling over, he wasn't sure what to think of what Tex had just told him—nor of the unusual sight before them.

10

It was one of the more incongruous sights Bud had ever seen.

The old rock structure at Temple Mountain, which had been the home of pack rats for many years and possibly even a few sidewinders, now sported a primitive handmade sign reading, *Espresso, Kombucha, Navajo Fry Bread.*

Bud didn't know what kombucha was and wasn't sure that he wanted to know, but he did know all about espresso, especially the coffee drink that had become known at his wife's Melon Rind Cafe as the Shumway Latte, which was coffee with a dollop of vanilla-bean ice cream and very popular.

Below that sign was another that simply read, *Temple Mountain Cafe.* Bud didn't know if the old rock building was on BLM land or not, but he suspected it was, making the enterprise illegal, just as Carl had suspected. He wondered who the proprietor was.

Bud noted the roof was now missing, a new development since he'd been there last. He asked Tex, "Where's the cafe?"

"Over here!" A voice replied just as Bud noted a small arrow pointing back across the wash. There, tucked under a huge cottonwood, sat a small aluminum trailer bearing the words *Bowlus Road*

Chief on its side. A dark-haired woman stuck her head out the door, saying, "Come over and I'll take your order."

Bud and Tex walked over to the trailer, the woman coming out and handing them each a handwritten menu that read, "*Espresso, Kombucha, Authentic Navajo Fry Bread, Authentic Navajo Tacos, Canned Pop & Cinnamon Rolls when available. Ask for prices.*

Bud noted that she wore blue jeans and a fleece hoodie and looked to be in her mid-thirties. Her thick hair was tied up in a knot on the back of her head, stray strands floating around her face like electrically charged sprites, and she had an air of someone who was used to being in charge, which seemed to contrast with an underlying gentleness.

Tex said, "Hi, Hattie. What are your prices today?"

"What exactly do you want, Tex?" The woman smiled.

Bud was surprised, as they obviously knew each other.

Tex replied, "Well, it depends on today's prices. Maybe a taco."

He turned to Bud, explaining, "The prices change depending on what Hattie gets charged for ingredients. Her nephew brings stuff over from Blanding."

Bud now thought he saw a moment of concern in her eyes when she recognized him.

"Hello Sheriff," she said quietly. "Tacos are $4.99."

"I'll have one," Bud said.

"I use authentic fry bread to make them," she said proudly. "It's an old Navajo recipe."

Now Tex said, "You don't look like an old Navajo."

Hattie replied, "I'm not."

Tex said, "You just said you were."

She looked confused. "No, I didn't. I said the recipe is Navajo. I got it from my mom."

"Well," Tex replied, "You don't look half-Navajo."

"I'm not."

Bud stood by, trying not to smile, knowing Tex was teasing her.

Tex said, "If your mom is Navajo, then you're half-Navajo."

Now beginning to look frustrated, Hattie replied, "I didn't say my mom was Navajo."

"You said the recipe was a Navajo recipe and you got it from your mom."

"That doesn't make my mom Navajo. She had a good friend she got it from who *was* Navajo, but she's Greek."

"So this is like false advertising, right?" Tex was now grinning mischievously.

"No, not at all. It's Navajo fry bread. I didn't say it was made by Navajos, it's just from an authentic Navajo recipe. Do I have to be Scottish to make shortbread, or Greek to make felafel?"

Tex asked, "How hard is it to make fried bread, anyway?"

"It's fry bread, not fried bread."

"But you do fry it, right?"

Now Hattie laughed, "You're just giving me a hard time, aren't you, as usual? You'd think I'd catch on one of these days. Do you want a taco or not?"

"I'll take two," Tex replied.

"And you, you want two also?" She asked Bud.

"No, one's enough. But I'd like a root beer with mine."

As Hattie went back inside, Tex said, "I've been in the outback too long."

"I thought you said you'd only been out there one day," Bud laughed.

Tex asked, "You know Hattie?"

Bud replied, "Yes, she's from Price. Her dad, Harry Kourlis, was a friend of my uncle. I'm surprised she remembers me, as she was just a kid last time I saw her."

"What do you know about her?" Tex asked.

"Not much, except she's running an illegal cafe."

"Does that make us criminals?"

"We're definitely enabling it."

"Are you going to shut her down?"

"I need to talk to her about it before the BLM comes out and tickets her. They're the ones who will shut it down, as it's their jurisdiction. But actually, she's also violating county and state laws unless she has food handler and business licenses, which I doubt."

"Well, a perfectly nice establishment ruined for no reason."

Just then, Hattie emerged from the small trailer with their tacos on paper plates. They sat down on rocks as she handed them their drinks.

Tex said, "Sorry for harassing you. I've been out in the sun too long."

"It's OK," Hattie replied. "What are you doing with the Sheriff? Did you finally get yourself in trouble?"

She laughed, but it seemed strained to Bud.

Bud bit into the taco, munching for awhile, then said, "Hattie, this is delicious. Why aren't you running a cafe up in Price or some place where there are actually people around?"

"This place was pretty busy until just recently," she replied. "Hikers and mountain bikers. I can't afford to rent a building up there and outfit it with a kitchen and tables and all that. But it's getting cold. I'm going to have to shut it down soon."

"Are you living out here?" Bud asked.

"Kind of. I go down to Goblin Valley at night. My friend works there and lets me stay with her. I was staying here in my trailer, but it's getting too cold. My friend's a ranger. But she'll be leaving soon, too. Everything kind of shuts down when it gets too cold, as you know."

Hattie now sat on a nearby rock. "To be honest, I have nowhere to go, so I'm staying as long as I can. Plus I desperately need any money I can make. Who knows when I'll have work again?"

"That's a shame, Hattie," Bud said. "No family up in Price anymore?"

"Nobody I want to stay with. Most everyone's died or moved away, gone over to the coal mines by Paonia in Colorado. The few left aren't close family. Besides, I'd be too embarrassed to ask for a handout. And my ex-husband..."

They sat in silence for awhile, eating their tacos, as Hattie ran her hands over Lindie's yellow coat, the dog looking at her with adoration.

Bud said, "That's Lindie. She sure seems to take to you."

"She's a neat dog," Hattie replied.

He continued. "Hattie, do you realize you're on BLM land here? Private enterprise is illegal. If they catch you, you'll get a hefty fine. They might even confiscate your trailer."

Hattie gasped. "Take my trailer? That's all I've got. But Bud, this is state lands, not BLM."

Bud said patiently, "No, I checked the maps, and it's definitely BLM. The nearest state lands are over on the road to Goblin."

Hattie stood and began pacing nervously.

"What can I do?" She finally asked.

"You're going to have to move," Bud replied. "You're also violating state health laws by not being licensed."

Hattie now looked like she might cry. "But I have no place to move to, and my old truck is starting to burn oil real bad. I have no idea what's wrong with it. I've really got myself in a pickle. It all started when I broke my ankle. Everything was fine until then."

Tex asked, "What about your nephew over in Blanding?"

"Oh, he's just a kid. He's going to the college there. He's as poor as I am. I pay him to bring me supplies, and I think it's the only money he ever has."

Bud stood, noting the sun was beginning to drop behind the cliffs.

"I have to go, but Hattie, you really need to get out of here. The BLM has to do their job. I'm going to give you some time before I can no longer look the other way regarding proper licensing and all that, but I have no idea when they might show up."

He turned to go, calling Lindie, then added, "I'm going to talk to my wife and see if we can't maybe put your little trailer on our farm until you can figure something else out. In the meantime, maybe Tex will hang around and see if he can see what's wrong with your truck —after all, he's an engineer. I guess you guys already know each other."

Tex replied, "I met her a few days before I went into the Maze."

Bud noted a small dirt bike parked next to the trailer.

"That's my Honda 250," Hattie said. "I like to go exploring."

"She's a good rider," Tex said.

"Well," Bud replied. "Give me a call when you can. I'll try to hold off the BLM to the best of my ability."

"I can look at your truck, Hattie," Tex offered. "But I might need some tools. I'll camp here by your trailer while you're over at Goblin, if that's OK. When do you come back in the mornings? I can help cook, too."

Hattie looked relieved. "I'm going to shut down the cafe in an hour, and maybe you can come check out my truck before I head out."

Bud smiled, adding, "I have a cherry pie for your cafe, Hattie. I know your customer Tex here wants some. My wife sells it for four dollars a slice back in Green River, and I think that's a fair price."

Hattie followed Bud over to his FJ, thanking him profusely, asking, "Are you sure you don't want a piece?"

"I need to watch my weight," he said, handing her a business card. "I just met Tex, but he seems like a good guy."

"He's really nice," Hattie replied. "But Sheriff..." She paused, and Bud waited, but finally she added, simply, "See you later," and walked back to the trailer.

Bud loaded Lindie up and started up his FJ, just as a group of mountain bikers rode up. As they eyed the pie, Bud could hear Hattie say, "Fresh, homemade, and four bucks a slice. And I have kombucha, too."

With that, he headed back to Green River, wondering what Hattie had been going to tell him and why she'd changed her mind.

11

Bud sat in his office, watching as Howie flipped through the pages of the *Lost Treasure Magazine* Bud had bought the other day at the Melon Harvest.

"You have any more of those Life Savers?" Howie asked.

Taking several from his pocket, Bud leaned back, handing a couple to Howie, then popping one in his mouth, reflecting on the conversation he'd just had with Carl, the BLM guy.

Bud had told him the proprietor of the cafe was in the process of moving, but he hadn't said exactly when. Carl thanked Bud for his help and asked him to keep him posted, and Bud could tell he seemed distracted, which he figured was a good thing.

Howie said, "Sheriff, this magazine's nothing like the old one. It's gone downhill, too much advertising. And the stories don't seem as authentic or something."

"The 50s were a special time for magazines, Howie," Bud replied. "Even into the 60s and maybe the 70s."

"How so?" Howie asked, rolling the Life Saver around in his mouth.

"It's hard to define, but it seems like the old ones had more of a sense of adventure or something. They looked at the world in a simpler way."

"And they weren't afraid to stretch the truth," Howie added. "Or even make stuff up. Nobody sued people back then. Everyone's afraid of their own shadows now."

"Well, Howie, that might be a good thing, you know," Bud replied. "Keeps people from libeling each other."

"Oh, I don't know," Howie said. "Old Man Green and Junkyard Goldie sure haven't slowed down any."

"What are they doing now?" Bud asked.

Howie replied, "Nothing new, just the same old same old, always accusing the other of something or other. Every time I run into them, they want me, as mayor, to fix something."

"Like what?" Bud asked, his feet now on his desk. He badly wanted to take a nap, but he knew Howie wouldn't let him, with his endless talk.

Howie continued. "Well, for example, the other day, Goldie called me and said he was being watched by the FBI and hadn't done anything wrong and wanted me to talk to them. When I asked how he knew he was being watched, he said that every time he logged onto the Internet he saw a wifi network that read *FBI Surveillance Van*."

Bud laughed. "That's an old joke people enjoy playing when they set up their network ID. What would be better is if you set it up to read, *Not an FBI Surveillance Van*."

Howie laughed. "I told him it was an old joke, Sheriff, but he didn't believe me. Said he was going to get you involved if I wouldn't do anything. Be forewarned."

Bud laughed, then closed his eyes. His stomach started growling, making him think about cherry pie, which brought him to the thought of Hattie out at the Temple Mountain Cafe. Wilma Jean had said it was OK to put the little trailer on the farm, but had added that Hattie would freeze to death if she tried to spend the winter in it, and they needed to find a better solution in the meantime. He would drive back down to Temple in the next few days and tell her, he thought.

He wondered if Tex had helped her figure out what was wrong with her pickup, then he began thinking about how maybe he could get Wilma Jean to make him a blackberry pie, his favorite, and how good it would be with vanilla-bean ice cream on it and why hadn't he ever thought to offer some to the dogs, maybe they'd like it, and was he being insensitive to eat it in front of them, and...

Bud woke with a start, his phone ringing. Almost tipping his chair over, he could hear Howie laughing as he managed to grab the edge of the desk.

"Sheriff's office, Bud speaking."

It was Marty, down at Green River Waterways.

"Bud, I need to report a missing raft and guide, a guy named Clint."

"The raft I can understand, but a guide?" Bud managed to say, still half-asleep.

"They kind of go together, Sheriff," Marty replied.

"How long have they been missing?"

"A couple of days now. This is a newer guide and he took a party of five down the river. They were supposed to come out at Mineral Bottom and get a ride with a shuttle back to Radium, where they would spend the night, then another shuttle would bring them back here. But nobody's heard anything from anybody since they left."

"And you're just now reporting them missing?" Bud asked.

"Bud, I've been busy closing things down for the season, as most of my help's already left. It was this guide's last day, so his not coming back is no big deal, though normally a guide would at least be in contact and tell us. And sometimes we have clients who, when they get to Radium, want to stay longer and see the sights there, and they usually contact us, too, but not always. The shuttle service holds our boats for us, but they said the group never showed up."

"Is it a yellow raft?" Bud asked, now awake.

"Yes."

"I think I know where it is. If it's the same one, it's tied up at Spanish Bottom."

"Spanish Bottom? That's on the Colorado, way past Mineral Bottom. What would they be doing down there?"

"Wandering around playing music, maybe," Bud replied.

"What?"

"Did they mention being part of an orchestra?" Bud asked.

"I have no idea," Marty said. "Maybe they missed the Mineral Bottom takeout and landed there instead. It's the final pickup spot before Cataract Canyon, but nobody would know to pick them up there if they hadn't prearranged it. But you definitely don't want to go on through Cataract. Fifteen miles of class III and IV big water rapids, and a two mile stretch of class IV to V big rapids in the middle. As you know, it can be a killer."

"Marty, can you take me down to Spanish Bottom in a jet boat tomorrow?"

"Sure, Bud, though it'll be a long day. I need to go get that raft anyway. What're you thinking?"

"I want to check out the fishing," Bud replied.

"Fishing out of a jet boat? Not while it's moving, I hope. Oh, wait, I get it. It's something you don't want to talk about. That's fine. Meet me at the state park around eight. Dress warm."

"Sounds good," Bud replied.

Lightly tapping his fingers on his desk, Bud suddenly felt as if he weren't doing his job properly. Sure, he'd had yesterday off and had helped Carl by going to Temple Mountain, but he'd been remiss by not contacting Green River Waterways to ask about that raft he'd seen while retrieving the oboist's body, even though he'd seen their lettering on its side.

It seemed obvious that it was the same raft he'd seen from high on the rim while watching the party in the wooden dories. Not many people rafted the Green this time of year, and the timing was right, and it did seem possible the oboist was one of the rafters. He recalled thinking at the time that it was probably a party on a day trip.

He turned to Howie to say something, then noticed he was fast asleep, chin on his chest, the magazine on the floor.

Bud got up and collected his jacket and cell phone, left Howie a note, then quietly slipped out the door.

Meet me tomorrow at the state park at eight if you want to go for a jet-boat ride, dress warm, be prepared to hike. Bud. P.S. Any word from the Chicago Symphony?

He hoped Howie could go along, for he wanted to climb up to the Dollhouse and look around, finish measuring stuff, and even though he intended to take Lindie, having Howie there would add a lot to his confidence level. He knew Marty would want to stay behind with his boat.

Bud knew he and Cal had been thorough, but they hadn't had time to really look around back in the hoodoos, and he wondered if there might be some kind of evidence they'd missed.

In any case, even though he wouldn't know the actual cause of death until the autopsy report came back, he didn't relish the idea of having a cold unsolved murder case in his files, and he vowed to figure out what had happened.

12

Bud knew that the noise of a jet boat irritated everything on the river, from the great blue herons and other waterfowl to the rafters and canoeists slowly floating along, but he still enjoyed the feeling of adventure that came with almost flying down the river, the scenery changing every moment as the boat ate up the river miles.

Lindie sat on the seat next to him, ears back, watching everything with what Bud felt must be a sense of wonder, since it was her first jet-boat ride. He knew she'd been on the water many times up in British Columbia, where she'd gone fishing with her previous owner on Lindeman Lake, which she'd been named after. Bud didn't worry too much about her jumping off, though he did have a hand on her shoulder harness.

Marty took the boat directly across a small rapid, the spray hitting Bud in the face, and he looked back to see how Howie was faring on the seat behind him. He looked distracted, not really paying much attention to the scenery, and Bud hoped he wasn't getting motion sickness or something.

"How's it going back there?" Bud yelled over the noise.

"Good, good," Howie yelled back. "It's inspirational."

Bud wasn't sure what Howie meant, as he'd never felt particularly inspired while riding a jet boat, so he yelled, "What's it inspiring, exactly?"

"I'm writing a song, Sheriff. The motion and noise is inspiring me."

Bud laughed. Just like Howie to be inspired by a trip down the river on a noisy jet boat.

"What's it about?" He yelled through the spray.

"I'm going to call it, *I'm Risking My Life on the Highway of Your Love.*"

Bud laughed, knowing it was the exact type of thing Howie liked to play with his band, Howie and the Ramblin' Road Rangers. And since Howie had based his mayoral race on the town having more fun, promising rockabilly concerts each Saturday night, he knew the band needed lots of new material.

They passed the yellow and ruby travertines of Crystal Geyser, and soon Bud could see the rounded cliffs of shale and siltstone that made up Dellenbaugh Butte above them, named for Frederick Dellenbaugh, the expedition artist and assistant photographer with John Wesley Powell's second expedition down the Green and Colorado rivers.

"This is where John Wesley Powell camped in July of 1869," Marty yelled back to them, pointing to a wide beach below the butte. "Some people call it the Anvil. It's Summerville Formation."

Bud had read about Powell's two expeditions down the mighty rivers in the mid-1880s, the first trip for exploration, and the second for geology and cartography. Powell himself had written two books about it, but Dellenbaugh, not quite eighteen when he was hired for the second trip, became famous for his account, *A Canyon Voyage*, proving himself a talented writer.

Marty continued, "Dellenbaugh told Powell the butte looked like an art gallery, so Powell named it for him. There are Indian ruins on the top of the butte, believe it or not. I have no idea how they got up there."

Bud knew Marty was used to guiding groups down the river, a

profession that required not just boatsmanship and people skills, but also a thorough knowledge of the history, geology, and even the flora and fauna. Bud had met boatmen who knew more about the river than some who had lived along it all their lives.

They passed Ruby Ranch and the confluence with the San Rafael River, and the Green soon began to twist and turn in huge meanders. They were entering what Powell had named Labyrinth Canyon, the smooth river now cut in two by their boat's wake, similar to places like Bowknot Bend where the river had almost cut the intervening cliffs in two. One could climb to a low saddle in the wall and watch the river run around the huge bowknot, arriving just a few hundred feet from the other side.

He knew this was one of the more pleasant stretches of the Green, bounded by giant cottonwoods, willows, cattails, and tamarisk, with nary a rapid along its entire stretch.

As they rushed downriver, the canyon became deeper and deeper, the massive orange, red, and gold Wingate Sandstone cliffs sometimes smooth, sometimes blocky, with peregrine falcon nests high above.

Soon they were passing June's Bottom, where Bud had once camped with the BOB-O's, the Bucket of Bolts Overlanders, who Eldon and Frosty led on forays that allowed vintage vehicles and equipment only.

Now next to Hell Roaring Canyon, Bud wished they had time to stop and hike to where the French-Canadian fur trapper, Denis Julien, had carved his name.

Even though the river was low, Bud knew that Marty could read it like the back of his hand, taking the boat back and forth across the waters to avoid hidden sandbars. They made good time, and even though it was almost 70 river miles from the Green River State Park, they were soon at Mineral Bottom.

Mineral Bottom was the standard takeout from Labyrinth Canyon and the put-in for Stillwater, the last stretch before the Green met the Colorado at the confluence, another 52 river miles.

Bud could now see that the river ramp held three wooden dories, their passengers milling about on the shore, watching as the jet boat drew nearer. Bud wondered again about the dory they'd seen down on Spanish Bottom. It had to be part of the group, but why was it so far ahead?

Marty slowed as the men on the shore began yelling and waving their arms for them to come ashore, then he yelled back at Bud, "No way." He then throttled the boat into high gear, leaving a foamy wake rocking the dories.

Bud wondered if they might need help of some kind, and he knew Marty carried a satellite phone, but he, too, was inclined to keep going, given their behavior toward the chopper.

Looking back, Bud could now see a man with one arm pushing various members of the group around as if trying to discipline them. The group settled down like a litter of contrite puppies just scolded by their mother and were soon out of sight, far behind.

So, the group had made it to Mineral Bottom, Bud mused. If they needed to, they could leave the river at that point on a twisty road that climbed up the cliffs onto the Island in the Sky, where surely a ranger or someone would give them a ride into Radium, assuming anyone would want to pick them up.

Wondering if Andy had gone through all the bags of Life Savers yet, Bud reached for one from his pocket. He was getting tired of the noise and the constant spray, and knowing they were only about halfway to the Dollhouse, he knew it was going to be a long day. They might even get back after dark, and though he knew the boat had powerful lights, he didn't relish the thought.

It was chilly, even with the November sun shining down on them, and he knew it would be downright cold after the sunset. He was glad for the warm coat he'd stuffed into his daypack.

Now Lindie, no longer finding the ride a novelty, lay down and put her head in Bud's lap, promptly going to sleep. Bud turned to look at Howie, who seemed lost in thought, watching the canyon walls get taller and taller.

They would soon be in the heart of Canyonlands National Park, at the confluence and then Spanish Bottom, where it's rumored the early Spaniards built the trail to the rim to search for gold.

And that's where they'd better stop, Bud mused, for there was no way he wanted to go in a jet boat—or any kind of boat, for that matter—down the treacherous rapids of Cataract Canyon.

13

Arriving at Spanish Bottom, Bud half-expected the yellow raft to be gone, washed from its mooring or even taken by its passengers, but it was still there, though now the dory was tied up closer to it. He could now make out the name *Cañonita* painted on the dory's side.

Marty beached the jet boat and Bud, Lindie, and Howie all jumped ashore, Bud going to the yellow raft. He wanted to thoroughly inspect it and see if it held any clues as to what had happened to the oboe player. He scrambled on board, but found it was completely empty except for its oars, as if someone had abandoned it.

Bud then jumped back out and walked all around the beach near the raft, looking for tracks, but it appeared that the winds had blown them away. Marty came over with a rope, and the three of them pulled the raft over to the jet boat, where Marty tied it to the rear of the boat for retrieval.

Bud and Howie next walked over to examine the wooden dory, noting how scuffed up and waterlogged the wood looked, even though it looked like someone had recently tried to seal it with some kind of resin. It appeared to have a slow leak, with a good half-inch of water in the bottom.

Though he felt reluctant to do so, Bud wanted to examine its contents. The group with the dories hadn't done anything illegal that he knew of, other than trying to poach geese, but Bud wanted to reassure himself they weren't up to something, plus he was curious as to what they were doing.

The problem was that the dory's contents, if it had any, were hidden in two hatches, one on each end, each secured with a leather cover. The long narrow boat had two wooden benches in the middle, and Bud sat on one as he managed to pull up the side of a cover enough to look under it with a small flashlight from his pocket.

The inside of the hatch was dark and musty and mysterious looking, filled with what appeared to be brass instruments one might use in surveying, which Bud recognized from his visit to the River Museum—barometers, chronometers, and sextants, along with sacks of flour, salt, coffee, beans, and bacon, and what looked to be ammunition, axes, hammers, saws, and augers.

He pulled the cover back down, saying to himself, "That's a rat's nest in there. It would take all afternoon to clean it out and figure out what it all is, and that's just one end of the boat."

He jumped out of the dory and back onto the beach, where Lindie was digging in the sand. Poking around with his boot, Bud found, of all things, an unwrapped peppermint Life Saver.

His first thought was of Andy. Had he brought the dory down the river, and if so, was he alone, or was there someone with him? Why had he left the rest of the gang back at Mineral Bottom? Had his boat gotten away from him somehow, or was he lost?

Was Andy aware that he was at the head of the tricky and dangerous Cataract Canyon, a place hard enough to run in modern rafts, yet alone in waterlogged wooden dories with leaky seams? And at the low cfs the Colorado was running, the rapids would be even worse, possibly ripping the bottom out of a boat.

Bud now began methodically walking back and forth on the beach, looking for tracks, wondering where the dory's crew had gone.

Suddenly, something strange caught his eye, and he stopped, hardly believing what he saw. There, deep in the sand, were three saucer-shaped impressions, each the size of the big pads he'd seen on the long chicken-like legs of the flying pod thing.

"Howie, come take a look at this," Bud called, taking out his pocket camera.

Howie was soon there, saying, "Looks like a UFO landed here, Bud. Not a real big one, but..."

"One heavy enough to sink down into the damp sand a ways and leave these impressions," Bud said. "I wonder when it landed."

Howie replied, "Bud, I was just kidding about a UFO. What do you think it could be, for real?"

"Well, you know we've been seeing this thing that Sammy thinks might be a gyrocopter. These impressions sure look like the pads it had on its feet. Keeps it from sinking in the sand."

Howie was now looking upwards into the blue sky that held the rims of the deep canyon apart.

"Gives me vertigo, Bud," he said. "But you know, we're out here in the middle of nowhere. I'm glad Marty has a sat phone in case we need help."

"Do you think we're going to get abducted, Howie?" Bud grinned.

Howie replied, "Maybe, but not by a UFO, but by one of those pirate guys. Isn't this one of their boats?"

"I think so, but why does the name *Cañonita* seem so familiar? Something's going on that I should be able to figure out, but it's just not coming to me. But where did whoever was in the boat go?"

Now Marty, up the beach a ways, whistled at them, then yelled, "Tracks over here going up to the Dollhouse."

Howie and Bud both hurried over to where Marty pointed to a set of tracks going through the sand, then up the steep trail.

"These are fresh," Bud said. "Only a few hours old at the most, and the right size for Andy."

"Who's Andy?" Marty asked. "And how can you tell they're fresh?"

"See that line along the beach where the river was higher— maybe from rain upriver last night? The sand's still damp in places, and tracks in sand like this will dry quickly, and the edges fall off as they dry," Bud replied. "But the edges of these tracks are still well-defined, so it's likely these tracks are very fresh. And Andy's one of the gang back there. We may run into him."

Bud now looked upwards, the canyon wall looming above, and he could make out a series of what looked like steps.

Marty, following his gaze, said, "Over 1,300 feet elevation in less than a mile. It's like climbing a hundred staircases, some of them steeper than a spiral one. A real workout. If you're going fishing up there, Sheriff, don't be gone long, because we have to get back before dark."

Bud nodded, then picked up his daypack and started up the trail, Lindie and Howie behind.

Now seeing what was involved, he wasn't sure he really wanted to hike up to the top, but his sense of duty drove him on. He needed to get up to the Dollhouse and see if he could figure anything out, and the day wasn't getting any longer.

14

Huffing and puffing, Bud finally stopped to take a break. Howie was close behind and didn't seem to be bothered by the elevation gain at all.

"You're in better shape than I am," Bud said, leaning against a rock. Far below, he could see the yellow raft tied behind the jet boat. At first he couldn't see Marty, then he finally saw what looked like someone stretched out on one of the jet boat seats as if taking a nap.

"I should've stayed down there and taken a nap, too," Bud remarked. "This is too much work."

"Agreed," Howie replied. "Why are we coming up here, anyway? Marty said something about fishing, but you're not a fisherman, Bud."

"I'd rather he didn't know about the death until we're ready for people to know. Everyone's a suspect in a case like this."

"Even me?" Howie asked, grinning.

"Especially you," Bud replied, starting back up the trail.

"You're just kidding, aren't you, Sheriff?" Howie asked with concern.

Now they topped out, and Bud stopped again to catch his breath. As they stood admiring the view of the river far below and the maw of the mysterious Cataract Canyon not far beyond Spanish Bottom, Lindie began growling.

Someone was coming down the trail! Before long, Bud could tell it was Andy, just as he'd predicted.

Telling Lindie to hush, Bud could see that Andy had a big smile on his face, obviously glad to see them.

"How ye daein?" He asked with his Scottish accent.

"Good, Andy. Nice seeing you again. How are you?"

"Am pure done in," Andy replied. "But you know you're not supposed to have dogs in the national park? Not that anybody out here would know the difference, 'cause there ain't nobody out here."

"She's a search and rescue dog," Bud replied.

"Who ya searchin' for, if you don't mind my asking?"

"Nobody in particular. We just bring her along in case someone turns up missing," Bud said. "But what brings you up here, Andy?"

"I been up and down this trail several times. I think it might be time for me to get off the river, but this way doesn't look very promising, like maybe it just goes on into the desert."

Bud replied, "There's a highway over there, but it's many miles away and there's no water between. Well, there are a few springs in the Maze, but they're intermittent and unreliable. It's not a place you really want to be hiking without a good map. But are you scouting on behalf of the rest of the crew or something?"

Andy grimaced. "Nae, the Major ran me off. But he'll be sorry."

Bud wondered what Andy meant, as it sounded a bit ominous.

"Sorry?"

"Yeah. I'm the cook. Probably the one man you'd miss the most if you ran him off."

"Do you mind if I ask why he ran you off?" Bud asked.

Andy frowned. "His arm popped out. He acted all surprised, asking me, 'Where'd that come from?' He didn't like it when I said he was like a salamander that grows its tail back, you know, regenerates it."

Bud was confused. "His arm popped out?"

"Never mind. He was mad 'cause I didn't stay in character. That's very important, you know—we all get lectures every night over dinner about stayin' in character, which ironically enough is out of character, 'cause nobody in the books ever talked about stayin' in character. But what made it worse was that I started laughing. He ran me off. You know, sometimes the hardest part of this trip is dealing with him. His leadership is so far behind he thinks he's in front. But he'll be sorry."

"Stay in character? Are you making some kind of movie or something?" Howie asked.

"Who'd want to watch our sorry arses?" Andy asked.

"What exactly are you guys doing, anyway?" Bud asked.

"If I told you, I wouldn't be staying in character," Andy replied. "But we need to get down off here before it gets dark. Let's go, fellas."

Bud hesitated. They hadn't even reached the Dollhouse, and yet the afternoon was wearing on. It had taken much longer than he'd expected to get there, even in a jet boat, and he'd known it was a long ways. Yet, he'd still underestimated it, and the Dollhouse itself was probably another 45 minutes away.

Knowing that Marty would be wanting to head back up the river, he nodded to Howie and began following Andy back down the trail.

He'd failed in his mission, but he knew another way to get back in here, one that would take longer but be much more enjoyable—he'd recruit Eldon and Frosty of the BOB-O's to come back down with him by road. But he knew they needed to come soon, for any evidence that might exist would soon be blown away by the desert winds, if it wasn't already.

Soon back down to the river, they boarded the jet boat, Andy looking at them wistfully from the beach.

"Is there a reason you can't go back out with us?" Bud asked.

"No, except integrity. There's still a lot of rapids to be run and stuff to be named. They'll be coming along here soon enough. I've decided to stay with the Major and see the project through."

"Project?" Bud asked, though he knew Andy wouldn't tell him, saying he had to stay in character.

"I can't tell you anything, because you actually don't even exist yet," Andy smiled, waving goodbye as they headed back upriver.

15

Bud sat in the back booth at the Melon Rind Cafe, eating a slice of warm cherry pie a la mode and wondering if Hattie and Tex had managed to get her old pickup fixed or at the very least, diagnosed.

Eldon, who was sitting across from him with Frosty by his side, said, "Bud, we need to get this trip organized if we're going out tomorrow. Any idea what the weather's going to do?"

Just then, Wilma Jean walked over, and sitting next to Bud, whispered, "You guys know who that fellow in the booth by the front door is?"

They all turned to look at the same time, and the guy nodded at them, smiling.

"Now he knows we're talking about him," Wilma Jean whispered with concern.

"What's going on?" Bud asked.

"Nothing, really, he's just asking everyone tons of questions. Maureen says he's harmless, but Wanda told me she's seen him all over town when she's doing her mail route, and he's interrogating everyone."

"Interrogating?" Howie asked. "As in FBI or something?"

"No, it's not like that, Howie," she continued. "It's not really personal stuff. He asks about everything under the sun, like what kind of toothpaste you use, what your favorite TV show is, that kind of thing."

"Toothpaste is pretty personal, in my book," Frosty replied. "I mean, it says a lot about you whether you use Crest or Tom's or baking soda."

"Like what?" Eldon asked.

"It's obvious, Eldon," Frosty replied. "If I use Tom's, it means I'm a little more on the green side than if I use Crest, and maybe even a little better heeled, as it costs more. And baking soda users are probably from the Depression—or hippies."

Eldon asked, "I wonder what kind of toothpaste celebrities use."

"Opalescence Whitening Toothpaste," Howie said.

Wilma Jean stood. "I can see you guys know less about him than I do."

"If he asks me any questions, I'll make his head spin," Eldon said. "Bud, you're the sheriff, go ask him what he's doing."

"Then *I'd* be the one prying," Bud answered.

"Ask him how they get the stripes in toothpaste," Frosty commented. "Do they still make that minty stuff called Pepsodent?"

Bud thought of the mint-flavored Life Savers Sherwyn had said could be bad for you. "Might want to stay away from that," he said. "Wintergreen can be bad if you get too much."

"Bud, mint and wintergreen aren't the same thing," Howie said. "And Pepsodent uses sassafras. Wintergreen is minty flavored, but they use a plant that's not a true mint. I think mints themselves are OK."

"Who told you that?" Bud asked.

Howie replied, "Sherwyn, down at the store. We had a long discussion about it. Very interesting stuff."

"You were trying to buy wintergreen Life Savers, weren't you, Howie?"

"You have any on you, Bud?"

Bud handed everyone a Life Saver as Wilma Jean went back into the kitchen.

Frosty remarked, "I quit using Pepsodent when I found out it had sugar in it. No point brushing your teeth to get rid of the sugar when there's sugar in the toothpaste."

Eldon replied, "Frosty, you told me that once before, so I looked it up, right on a tube of Pepsodent. There's no sugar—it's saccharin."

"Same thing."

"No, it's not," Eldon replied. "But can we get back on track here, boys? Bud wants to go down to the Maze tomorrow. Anyone checked the weather?"

Bud could see the fellow in the front booth turn, as if listening.

"I did, and it looks good," Frosty said. "But we'd better not delay, as it'll be winter before you know it."

"It won't be winter that soon. Just how long do we need to supply for?" Eldon asked.

"Maybe a couple of days," Bud replied. "I want to go down to the Dollhouse. We'll swing over to Temple Mountain on the way, which will add an hour or two."

"What's at Temple?" Frosty asked.

"The Temple Mountain Cafe. We can go get a taco. I need to check up on the owner."

"There's a cafe over there now?" Eldon asked with surprise. "Since when?"

"I don't know," Bud replied. "But I do know it's not going to be open much longer."

"Winter's coming," Frosty said.

Eldon stood to go, saying, "Well, we ain't gettin' any younger sittin' around. Let's get supplied up. I need to get some groceries."

"Is this an official BOB-O's expedition?" Howie asked. "'Cause if it is, I can't go. I don't have an old enough vehicle."

"All our expeditions are official BOB-O's expeditions, Mayor," Eldon replied. "Why not ride with Bud?"

"That's fine," Bud said, sliding out of the booth. "But Howie, your old RV would qualify. I need to get a few groceries, too. So we'll meet at eight tomorrow at the park, right?"

"Yup," Eldon replied, heading toward the door.

As he walked by, the man in the front booth stood and held out his hand, saying, "I'm Phil Baker. You guys going to play some kind of video game or something? I heard you mention the Maze."

Eldon stopped, Frosty behind him, and shook the man's hand. "I'm Eldon and this is Frosty, and that's Bud and Howie. Nope, we're going to a real maze."

"Oh," the man replied, seeming impressed. "I knew they grew corn here, but I didn't know there was a maze. Where is it?"

Eldon didn't miss a beat. "It's a ways to the south."

"I don't mean to be forward, but I'm here on vacation," Phil said. "I don't know anything about this area. Do you enjoy going to mazes? And what was this talk about the BOB-O's?"

Eldon guffawed. "Everyone likes mazes. We're the BOB-O's, the Bucket of Bolts Overlanders. The rules for the BOB-O's state that you can only use equipment at least 25 years old, and that includes your clothes and camping gear, though your food doesn't have to be old."

"You know, like the good old days," Frosty added.

"It must be a really big maze to take a couple of days," Phil added.

"Oh, it is," Eldon replied. "The biggest one you'll ever see."

"Can I get there in my rental car, a Ford Focus?"

"You can ride with Bud," Eldon said.

Bud groaned. He hadn't told Eldon and Frosty why he wanted to go to the Dollhouse, and having an uninvited and unknown guest along could complicate things, especially if the guy rode with him and Howie. They wouldn't be able to talk about the case or investigate things like he wanted.

Eldon was famous for his generosity when it came to taking people out in the backcountry, and many a stranger had found themselves half-unprepared and at the mercy of the BOB-O's, but Bud didn't know anyone who hadn't seemed to enjoy it.

Everyone in Green River knew about the BOB-O's, and probably half the residents had been on at least one expedition through the years. A lot of them would loan out gear to friends and family who wanted to go.

Now outside, Bud pulled Eldon aside and said, "I need to have you take Phil with you. Howie and I are doing some investigative work out there—mum's the word—and we can't have a complete stranger in on it."

"You should've said something, Bud," Eldon said.

"Well, it was supposed to be low key. I didn't know you were going to ask a guest along," Bud replied. "I'd prefer nobody knew why we're going out there."

Eldon looked irritated. "Just why *are* you going out there? I thought we were going to see the country and enjoy ourselves."

"Nothing will stop us from doing that," Bud replied. "I just need to look around the Dollhouse. I can fill you in on it later, but right now mum's the word."

"Loose lips sink ships. My lips are sealed," Eldon replied.

"And I'd actually prefer not to do the BOB-O's thing this time," Bud added. "It's going to be a work trip, and I may need to talk to a few people, and I don't want to be dressed like someone out of a time capsule."

"Who would you talk to down in the Maze?" Eldon asked.

"You never know," Bud replied. "But I may have to convince someone I'm the sheriff, and wearing orange plaid pants might wreck my credibility. But you guys can come in style."

"Whatever floats your boat, Sheriff," Eldon replied. "But this Phil guy is up to something, and taking him along with us, well, he'll be sure to spill the beans over a warm campfire after a couple of shots of whisky."

"Very considerate of you to look out for the folks of Green River like that, Eldon," Bud said.

"Somebody's got to do it," Eldon replied. "And not to worry, I'll keep him away from your investigating, whatever it is."

"Much appreciated," Bud said. "See you in the morning."

16

"I'm going to take it out for its inaugural run, Sheriff, it's very first trip under my new ownership," Howie said, patting the hood of his old RV at the city park, where they'd agreed to meet.

Eldon looked on approvingly, "It is over 25 years old, isn't it?"

"It sure looks like it," Frosty added.

"It is," Howie confirmed. "In fact, it's even older than that—it's 30. I got the alternator fixed, then I spent yesterday afternoon cleaning it all up and stocking it with all kinds of stuff—sleeping bags, hotdogs, my old cast iron skillet, my lantern, plastic forks and spoons, chips, soda..."

"It's a dandy," Eldon said. "But you can't take something that big and tippy down the Golden Stairs. The wheel base is too long—you'll get high centered if you don't roll the darn thing first."

"I'm going to leave it at the top. We can use it as a base camp. I'll be living in luxury while you guys sleep on the ground."

"Not me," Frosty said. "I'm too old and stoved up for that. I have a cot."

"Is your cot at least 25 years old?" Bud grinned.

"Close enough," Frosty replied. "And my knees are more than old enough."

"So, what's our game plan, boys?" Eldon asked, looking around at everyone's clothing. He himself was dressed in his usual BOB-O's garb, a tan polyester stretch leisure suit that made him look like he came straight from the lounge at the old defunct Country Club Nightclub. Frosty wore an old pair of bell-bottom jeans and a t-shirt with the words, "KOAL, Voice of Castle Country, Price, Utah."

Bud was sure Howie had simply put on one of his Ramblin' Road Rangers sequined jackets, and even though it was fairly new, it could've easily been something seen on a TV variety show some 25 years back.

Phil, the guy from the diner, hadn't shown up, and Bud wondered if he'd decided the bunch wasn't a bit too eccentric for his tastes.

"Your fashion sense is a little glitzy," Eldon commented to Howie. "You're going to shine like a beacon out in the desert sun. No worries about getting lost and having people find you when you wear gold sequins."

"It's all I had," Howie said defensively. "Besides, I need to write some songs for our rockabilly concerts, and wearing this inspires me."

"You gonna start writing Elvis-style songs?" Frosty asked.

"Elvis wore gold lamé, not sequins," Eldon corrected. "He was a polyester kind of guy."

"Actually, Eldon, he wore jumpsuits, just like you've got on," Frosty said.

"It's not a jumpsuit, it's a leisure suit."

"Fellas, we need to get going," Bud interrupted. "If we get separated, meet me at Temple Mountain. Maybe I should follow you, Howie, just in case you break down."

They were soon on the road to Hanksville, and following Howie, Bud could see that the old RV bounced with every bump as if needing new shocks. Bud kept his distance, wondering if something might come flying off it if Howie got going much faster.

He noted that with Eldon in the lead, followed by Frosty, then Howie, then him with Lindie, it looked like a convoy. They even had

CB radios so they could communicate. Keying his on, Bud said, "Don't forget to turn at Temple Mountain. Over."

"That's a Roger, good buddy, 10-4," Eldon replied.

"10-4," Frosty added, then Howie said, "10-4."

"You fellas don't have to all 10-4 me," Bud laughed. "I assume we're all following Eldon."

They soon turned on the Temple Mountain Road, now going west. As they drove along, Bud wondered if Howie had heard any more from the orchestra people. If it weren't for the dead oboe player, he would write it off as a prank, but now he wasn't so sure.

He could soon see something shining in the near distance, and as they got closer, he recognized Hattie's old aluminum trailer. It sat next to the road, just before the turnoff to Goblin Valley, and her old pickup was parked nearby, her dirt bike loaded in its bed.

Good for her, Bud mused, knowing it was all now on state lands and in no danger of being shut down, at least not by the BLM. Bud guessed that Hattie was still illegal, but the state was well-known for not paying much attention to its many sections of trust lands.

"Pull over at that old trailer coming up," Bud said over the CB.

"10-4," everyone replied.

As they stopped, Bud looked on in amazement, for the trailer now looked like a genuine roadside cafe. He could see that the large placard with the menu had been redone, with wraps, burritos, and salads added. Several sets of folding picnic tables and chairs sat in front, each sporting a red tablecloth and vases with artificial daisies.

As they pulled over, Tex emerged from beneath the pickup, wiping his hands on a rag.

"Bud! Nice seeing you. I just finished changing the oil."

After introducing everyone, Bud asked, "Did you figure out what was wrong with the truck?"

"It needs new rings, something I can't do, but at least we know now what's wrong," Tex replied. "How do you like our new setup? Man, we're keeping busy. Even though it's basically the end of the season, we're getting the traffic going to Goblin, which Hattie wasn't getting before, tucked up under Temple Mountain. I've been going into Green River for supplies. I wanted to look you up, but we've been so busy..."

Hattie emerged from the trailer, saying, "Great seeing you, Bud, and there's that sweetheart Lindie. You guys hungry?"

"You're on state lands now, Hattie. Good move," Bud replied. "I'd like one of those delicious tacos and a root beer."

They all ordered, and Tex and Hattie went inside the trailer, Hattie soon emerging with their food. Bud noticed that Tex's tent was again pitched behind the trailer.

"I have to go get supplies," Tex said. "I'll see you guys later." He was soon gone in Hattie's old truck, blue smoke billowing out the exhaust.

"How long are you going to stay out here?" Bud asked Hattie, Lindie hanging out under the table, hoping he would slip her a few bites.

"As long as possible," Hattie replied. "We're doing really well, and with Tex able to get supplies and help out, things are going great. And we have a new regular customer. He comes by every day and orders tons of food."

Bud was curious, knowing nobody lived nearby, except for those down at Goblin State Park.

"A park employee?" He asked.

"No, I'm not sure where he lives or anything, but he comes in and orders a couple dozen tacos, drinks, salads, and cinnamon rolls—I've sold him a gazillion cinnamon rolls—and coffee..."

"He must be a guide or something feeding clients. Nobody lives around here except at Goblin," Bud replied.

Hattie replied, "We have a standing order for him every day. He's actually our main customer."

"That's great," Bud said. "But do you have any idea who he is?"

"No, though you should ask Tex, as he knows him."

She then pulled a pen from her pocket, saying, "He did leave this on a table the last time he was here. I was going to return it to him, next time he comes in."

She handed Bud a silver metal pen with lettering on it as she added, "Keep it if it's helpful."

Bud looked at the pen. It bore the words, *Picco Avionics, Chicago Executive Airport, Wheeling, IL.*

He recalled the business card he'd found in the oboe player's suit —hadn't it read *George Picco, Picco Avionics*? Bud knew it had to be the same person.

Hattie set to clearing the nearby tables, but was soon back at Bud's side, saying, "One thing you might want to know, I've had a few customers come in saying they've been hearing music in the canyons."

Bud wondered if this was what she'd been hesitant to tell him last time he'd seen her. "Music? What kind of music?"

"Classical, like an orchestra. I find it kind of odd."

"Yes, it is odd. Did anyone say where exactly?" Bud asked.

"One guy said he heard it in Crack Canyon, and a pair of mountain bikers said they heard it clear over in Red Canyon."

"Those aren't very close to one another."

"They just said they were playing classical music. Everyone really liked it, said it was beautiful, though it was really strange. Probably someone with a really loud speaker on their car stereo."

"Not in Crack Canyon," Bud replied. "You can drive through Red Canyon, but Crack Canyon is a slot, like Little Wildhorse. Do you have any ideas what it could be?"

"Not really," she replied.

For some reason, Bud felt she was dodging again. He wondered why she'd brought it up if she didn't want to discuss it. It was almost like she wanted to tell him something else but was afraid to.

Noticing everyone was finished and waiting for him, Bud said, "We need to get going, Hattie. Thanks for the tacos." He paused, then added, "And by the way, when you decide you're ready, my wife says it's fine for you to put your trailer on our farm, though she's worried you'll freeze to death in it. But we'll work something out."

Hattie smiled. "Tell your wife I'm so grateful. I'll make it up to you guys somehow."

Bud replied, "She has a cafe, and maybe she can use your help somehow. She would pay you, of course. The farm's free, no rent, but you'll be wanting something more permanent when it gets colder."

Bud loaded Lindie up and followed Eldon and the gang back down the Temple Mountain Road. They again joined the highway to Hanksville, but soon turned east onto the dirt road to the Hans Flat Ranger Station.

Still last in the convoy and eating everyone's dust, Bud suddenly felt a sense of foreboding, knowing they would soon enter the maw of the mysterious and untrodden Maze. He leaned over and patted Lindie, saying, "Everything's gonna be OK," as if reassuring her, though he knew he was really reassuring himself.

As they drove along, Bud again thought of the oboe player, wondering what had happened to him and if Hum and Cal had an autopsy report yet. Even though Cal had said he'd probably just fallen and hit his head, Bud knew it hadn't been an accident, given the way he'd landed on his back.

And whoever had killed him could still very easily be out there in those mysterious depths, waiting.

17

After driving across a blackbrush flat for many miles, it was late afternoon when they finally arrived at the Hans Flat Ranger Station, where Eldon pulled over, everyone following suit. Bud got out and went inside, greeting the park ranger.

"How's your day going, Cynthia?" He asked.

"Why, it's Sheriff Shumway!" Cynthia answered in surprise. "What brings you to these parts?"

She then lowered her voice and added, "We heard about the death out in the Maze. I assume you're looking into it?"

"Cynthia, have you heard or seen anything unusual before or since then?"

"Not really," she replied. "Just a few day-hikers, and they're getting few and far between this time of year."

"Is Gary in Radium?"

"No, he's down in Horseshoe Canyon leading a tour down to the Great Gallery. They should all be back soon."

"I figured there wouldn't be any more tours this late in the season," Bud replied. He'd been down at the Great Gallery several times and always stood in awe of the life-sized rock art figures with their intricate designs, considered to be some of the most significant pictographs in North America.

"It's a last-minute thing, a group that's here from somewhere back in the Midwest."

"How many?"

"I'm not sure, maybe a half-dozen. I didn't actually see them, as he was going to meet up with them out on the rim. Where are you guys headed?"

"We need a permit to camp at the Dollhouse, Cynthia. I think we'll camp at the top of the Golden Stairs tonight, then at the Doll-house tomorrow night."

She waved her hand in dismissal. "If you're doing an investiga-tion, you don't need a permit, and you're not in the park yet at the Golden Stairs, you're still in the Glen Canyon National Recreation Area and can camp anywhere you want. But you do need a reserved campsite at the Dollhouse."

"Give us whichever is open and closest to the Dollhouse itself," Bud said.

"I'll block out #1 for tomorrow night. But we have some weather coming in a few days from now, so you'll be wanting to get back out before that. You know those steep switchbacks of the Golden Stairs are impassible when they're wet—bentonite clay all the way. We've had two vehicles slide off and need to be towed out so far this year, and I know it cost the owners a fortune, not to mention banged-up vehicles. You're of course aware you'll never get that big RV in there, aren't you?"

"That's why we're going to camp with it at the top of the Stairs. We'll leave it there for our second night, and Howie will ride in my rig down to the Dollhouse. Thanks, Cynthia. I'll stop on our way back out."

"Please do, so we know you're not still in there needing a rescue. And be careful going down the Flint Trail. Those switchbacks can be pretty gnarly, too. But I don't think we'll be here, as we're going into Radium for supplies, so just leave a note. And you know you can't have fires any more in the park, though you can at the Golden Stairs if you have your own wood."

She stopped, thinking, then said, "But Sheriff, I did see something odd, in fact, I saw it several times. There's some kind of weird flying craft that we see every so often out over the Maze."

"Kind of looks like an egg with chicken legs?"

Cynthia laughed. "It actually does, though I wouldn't have thought to describe it like that. I take it you've seen it?"

"It's making the rounds, but I have no idea what or who it is. Someone said maybe a gyrocopter, whatever that is."

Cynthia paused, then added, "One last thing. I just remembered that Gary and I were coming back from Horseshoe Canyon when we saw someone on a dirt bike in the distance going out toward the highway. We don't get many solo bikers, especially this time of year. No idea who it was, and they may have tried to check in at the station, but we'd closed it for the day. They were sure making good time, almost recklessly fast."

"Do you recall exactly when this was?" Bud asked.

"I'm not sure, but it was about when we heard about the dead guy. And then we had a guy come into the station in pretty bad shape about the same time the fellow died out in the Maze. This guy said he was a tourist just visiting and had gotten himself stuck on the road past Horseshoe. Said he'd come down the River Road all the way from Green River. He'd hiked a good six miles in flip-flops, so we took him back out to check out his rig to see what needed to be done. Usually we can pull people out."

She shook her head, then continued. "He was about as stuck as you can get, not to mention unprepared, but we did manage to get him out, and when we followed him, he got stuck a couple more times. I have no idea how he got out that far in the first place. He was lucky we could help him. I couldn't believe anyone would take a Ford Focus out here, especially since he said it was a rental."

"A rental?" Bud asked. "Did he bombard you with questions the whole time?"

"Do you know him?" She asked. "Yes, and they were really

strange, like what brand of boots we wear, how we decorate our house, stuff like that. It was odd. We got him back here, and he took off as if nothing unusual had happened, like he got stuck every day."

"Maybe he does," Bud replied. "He's been hanging around Green River. Did you get his name?"

"Yes, we filed a report. Let me find it."

Cynthia retrieved some paperwork from a file, then said, "His name was Phil Baker. He's from Chicago."

Bud wrote down the guy's address, then thanked Cynthia and turned to go, just as she let out a groan and pointed out the window, saying, "I can't believe this."

Bud watched as a white Ford Focus pulled up to the ranger station. A small wiry guy got out, dressed in a shiny oversized double-breasted gray herringbone suit. He also wore a black fedora with a gray band and a bright red tie.

He opened the door, and over a big cigar in his mouth, mumbled, "Sorry I'm late. It took me awhile to find an outfit. And don't worry, Ranger Cynthia, I'm riding with these guys."

Seeing Bud eyeing his obviously fake diamond pinky ring, Phil added, "We gangsters wear these pinky rings as a source of funding for our funeral expenses in case we're shot."

Bud tried not to laugh, while Cynthia just looked mystified.

Seeing their reactions, Phil added, "What? Eldon said I had to dress in clothes over 25 years old in order to come on a BOB-O's trip. A gangster from the '20s is way older than that. I had to go all the way up to Price to find all this stuff."

Bud groaned, said goodbye to Cynthia and followed Phil out the door, pretty sure he knew what Eldon and Frosty would say.

18

"So, do you prefer hot cereal or cold?" asked Phil, leaning against the stump of a juniper tree that Bud figured had long ago been sacrificed to someone's campfire by one of the cowpunchers or sheepmen who once ranged stock in this part of the canyon country.

Bud wondered if it had been cut down by Ernie Larson himself, the namesake of Ernie's Country, a vast maze of fins and washes and rugged canyons that had once been the stomping grounds of the man who'd run sheep there in the 1900s. The canyon country was rumored to have held tall bluestem grasses back then, long before things had started to dry up.

They were now camped just above the Golden Stairs, where the road fell off the rim into the vast canyons below into the Land of Standing Rocks. It had been a long day getting there, longer than had been necessary, since Howie's old RV had struggled with the ups and downs of the road, slowing them down.

They'd come down what was known as the Flint Trail, called that from the numerous scatterings of flint chips left in the area by natives when they made points for their spears and arrows. Archaeologists had no idea why they'd hauled the flint up from some 1,000 feet below, but Bud wondered if it weren't to enjoy the views while they flintknapped.

The Flint Trail was the main access into the roads of the Maze District, roads primarily created from 1949 to 1955 by prospectors during the Uranium Boom. A few remote backcountry airstrips still existed from that era, some kept up by backcountry pilots who enjoyed flying into the area to camp or to just test their skills landing on the rough strips.

The trail technically started at the Flint Trail Overlook, where it dropped down the brilliant Orange Cliffs from Hans Flat into what the old-time stockmen called the Under the Ledge Country. The road was called a trail because it had originally been just that, a narrow place where cowboys and sheepmen could push stock down Under the Ledge for grazing, using the few springs in the area for water. Of all the Maze area, only Jasper Canyon hadn't seen grazing, and it was now closed to the public as a study area.

Everyone seemed hesitant to drive down the steep road, and they all stood at the top for awhile, admiring the sweeping view into Ernie's Country, with a rugged area known as the Fins to its north side. To the south they could see the dark gorge of Cataract Canyon, far away, the Colorado River unseen at its bottom, hidden by tall canyon walls.

The Flint Trail had been improved somewhat by uranium miners, but not much, dropping 800 feet in the first mile with very few places wide enough for two cars to pass, so Bud had scoped it out as best he could for any vehicles that might be coming up before they all started down. He knew the switchbacks of the Flint Trail were steep, but nothing like those of the Golden Stairs.

Finally, they started down, having to make a couple of three-point turns on several very sharp and exposed sections, and Bud had wondered if Howie would make it down in his old RV. Once at the bottom, he wondered if he'd make it back up. There, the road split, and they'd made sure to go to the left, for going right would take one clear down to Hite on a road suitable for passenger cars, unless it had washed out from recent flashfloods.

They kept going until they'd finally made it to the top of the second set of switchbacks at the Golden Stairs, and as they set up camp, Howie walked back and forth, looking down, trying to convince himself that his old rig could make it. After all, it had made it down the Flint Trail switchbacks, so why not?

It seemed he'd just realized that if he left it where they were now, as he'd originally planned, he would also have to leave most of his gear and food and whatnot, including the small library of books he'd discovered in the back of one of its dusty cupboards. Among them was a copy of *The Wind in the Willows,* and he was carrying it around, caught up in the story of the Mole and Rat and their friends.

His tent now pitched, Bud was now trying to dissuade Howie from trying the Golden Stairs, as he knew the old truck could never make it down the steep and narrow switchbacks, and even if it somehow miraculously did, there was no way they could get it back up the steep cliff, a climb of over 800 feet in two miles with lots of shelf rock and sand. He knew it would be a challenge for the engine to pull the weight up the slippery and tippy rocks, and the almost-bald tires didn't look up to the job, either.

Bud had brought several bundles of wood, and he soon had a good fire going. Hungry, they ate their dinners of canned pork-and-beans and hotdogs, with Jello Surprise from the Melon Harvest for dessert (the surprise being the walnuts, which Bud hated and carefully picked out). The night sky began to open above them with its immeasurable points of light as the dying fire flung sparks upward in what seemed to be a salute.

"Are you making breakfast in the morning?" Frosty asked Phil. "Is that why you want to know what kind of cereal we prefer?"

Phil replied, "No, just wondering."

Eldon asked, "Why do you keep asking these irrelevant questions? Are you working up a personality profile on each of us or something?"

Phil snorted. "That would be something else—the shrinks would have a field day. But I'm just a curious kind of guy. My brain works that way."

"Your brain must be stuffed with useless information," Frosty said, kicking at a small stick that had caught on fire just outside of the fire ring.

Eldon added, "That cigar's gonna fall apart if you keep mouthing it like that. Just smoke it, for cryin' out loud. Why don't you ever ask anything of importance?"

"Like what?" Phil asked. "OK, how about this. Which baseball team do you think's gonna win the nationals?"

"You mean the Washington Nationals?" Frosty asked.

"He means the World Series," Howie replied. "The Washington Nationals are a baseball team."

Phil continued. "OK, so I know nothing about baseball. How about this—what do you think the future holds?"

Eldon snorted, saying, "I try to live for today."

Frosty replied, "Winter's coming, and there will be lots of snickerdoodles."

Phil sounded surprised. "Snickerdoodles, as in cookies?"

Frosty said, "Yeah, Eileen's a good cook. Those are my favorite."

Eldon groaned.

"Who's Eileen?" Phil asked.

Eldon said testily, "He's getting married in a couple of weeks. Let's change the subject."

"Congratulations!" Phil said.

Changing the subject, Eldon said to Howie, "I can't believe you want to take that RV down the Golden Stairs."

"It'll be kind of tricky," Howie said. "And more than a bit scary."

Bud laughed. "Wait until we try to get it back out."

Howie replied, "I was kind of thinking about maybe just leaving it down there."

Frosty sounded concerned. "You don't want the park having it towed out. They'll charge you a fortune. You may just have to part it out and take out the pieces one at a time. But we could hide it behind one of the hoodoos and use it for a vacation home. Eileen and I could have our honeymoon here."

Now Eldon, who'd apparently been chafing at the bit to say something to Phil and could no longer hold back, said, "By the way, Phil, that's the most ridiculous outfit I've ever seen. A gangster in the canyon country? Did you bring anything else to put on?"

Phil replied, "My pajamas."

"Gangsters never went camping," Eldon said with disgust.

Frosty countered, "Sure they did—when they were on the run. They probably camped out a lot."

Eldon said, "Hiding in the bushes ain't camping. Look, the BOB-O's mission is to re-create the good old days. How could gangsters be part of the good old days? They're part of the bad old days."

Frosty argued, "Think of Bonnie and Clyde robbing a bank—having all that cash, that would be a good old day to me."

"Till you got yourself shot," Eldon said, then turned back to Phil. "Ridiculous. That pinky ring is about as tacky as it gets. Next time, wear something more appropriate."

Phil laughed, nodding at Eldon's garb. "Like an Elvis leisure suit?"

Howie now chimed in, trying to prevent an argument. "Asking about what the future holds, well, my future holds a rockabilly concert next weekend. I just wrote a new song for it. Want to hear it?"

Bud said, "Sure. Where's your guitar?"

"In my rig. I'll go get it."

As Howie was retrieving his guitar from the RV, Phil asked, "Is he some kind of musician?"

"He has a rockabilly band—Howie and the Ramblin' Road Rangers," replied Frosty.

"And he's also the mayor?" Phil asked.

Howie was soon back, and after tuning his guitar, he began singing.

I'm risking my life on the highway of your love,
A hundred miles an hour and it ain't fast enough.
With pedal to the metal on the throttle of your heart,
If my alternator falters I'll be needing a jumpstart.

The highway of your love,

The highway of your love,
I'll stay out of the borrow pit with help from above.

You ran over my heart and now it's hanging off your
    bumper,
You're in a Maserati and I'm driving an old clunker,
My nerves are all a wreck and I can't slow down,
There's a speed trap waitin' at the edge of town.
I don't know what I'll do when I run out of gas,
It's gonna happen soon 'cause I'm driving way too fast.
That trooper right behind me he keeps flashin' his red
    lights,
And I know I'll be sleepin' behind bars for a few
    nights.

The highway of your love,
The highway of your love,
I'll stay out of the ditch with help from above.

After he'd finished, there was a moment of silence, then Eldon
said, "They say that for every piece of art, there's some suffering. And
that's all I'm gonna say about that."

Frosty replied, "Don't listen to him. That's good old country
music. The soundtrack to our lives. Lots of musicians reach for that
golden ring, but you nailed it, Howie. So simple, so deep."

Howie, looking embarrassed, replied, "Maureen told me I must've
made a pact with the Devil concerning my music. I was hurt at first,
then she said she didn't know what *I* got, but the Devil got guitar
lessons."

Everyone laughed as the fire burned down, almost gone, nothing
but a few embers dancing on a bed of ashes.

Eldon, maybe feeling bad about his earlier comment, said, "That
song should be enshrined in country music along with Johnny Cash's
A Boy Named Sue."

Howie, looking even more embarrassed, said, "It'll be better when Bud learns it on his harmonica, right, Bud?"

Now Phil, looking pensive, added, "It's a direct look into people's hearts and pulls no punches at what makes us human. Well done, amigo. But anyone have an idea where I can lay out my sleeping bag? I wasn't able to find an old tent."

"Watch out for them scorpions," Eldon cautioned.

"You can sleep in the RV cab," Howie offered. "It's plenty big enough."

They all sat silent around what was left of the fire, then, one by one, got up and wandered off to their tents.

Bud, settled down in his warm sleeping bag with Lindie snuggled at his side in her own bag, could hear Phil and Howie talking softly, then he heard the sound of Howie's pickup door closing, and all was quiet.

For a brief moment, he thought he heard the strains of classical music coming from the depths of the Maze, maybe something by Mozart, but deciding it was just the power of suggestion, he soon drifted off, the night sky dazzling in its silent infinity of stars.

19

After a breakfast of pancakes and hot coffee and yet more talk, Eldon and Frosty had finally headed back to civilization, Phil riding with Eldon back to the ranger station, where he would retrieve his rental car, getting schooled in the way of the desert rat by Eldon along the way, Bud figured.

They'd originally planned on going down to the Dollhouse with Bud and Howie, but Frosty had discovered a leak in his differential, and after much discussion, had decided it would be prudent to head back early. Bud was half relieved, knowing they wouldn't interfere with his investigation, nor would he need to explain himself.

Leaving the old RV at the top of the Golden Stairs, Howie rode with Bud and Lindie in Bud's FJ, having thrown his overnight stuff and guitar onto the back seat. As they made the long treacherous descent down the Golden Stairs, Howie thumbed through the copy of *The Wind and the Willows* he'd found in the RV.

"Are you trying to avoid watching the road?" Bud grinned. "It *is* kind of scary."

"I had bad dreams last night about the Flint Trail, Sheriff," Howie replied. "I have no idea how I'm going to get my rig back up that."

"I should've used executive privilege and had you park at the top there, instead of at the Stairs," Bud said.

"Don't you have to be president to have executive privilege?" Howie asked. "But have you read this?" He thumped the cover of the book.

"I think so, back in school," Bud replied. "It's about a water rat who decides to go traveling, if I recall."

"A boatman?"

"No, a real rat."

"There's real water rats, as in animals?"

"I guess so. It's British. I have no idea what they have over there."

"Lots of royal this and that," Howie replied. "Not exactly my cup of tea. But that rat must be Ratty. There's also Moley and Toady and Badger. Listen to this, Sheriff. It says on the back cover that President Teddy Roosevelt wrote to its author, Kenneth Grahame, to tell him that he had 'read it and reread it, and have come to accept the characters as old friends.'"

Howie was silent for awhile, reading, as Bud slowly continued down the rough road, passing a sign that read *Entering Canyonlands National Park*, with symbols indicating no ATVs, no campfires, no pets, and no hunting.

"Is Lindie going to get in trouble with the rangers?" Howie asked, looking up.

"No," Bud replied. "If anyone does, it'll be me. But Cynthia and Gary are the only rangers down here, and they know she's a search and rescue dog."

They continued on, now crossing the head of Teapot Canyon, a section some considered the toughest in all of Canyonlands, rocky and having long stretches of sandstone that could be slick when wet. Bud took his time, Lindie now asleep in the back in spite of the rocking of the FJ.

"Listen to this, Sheriff," Howie said, reading from the book as they bounced along.

A hundred bloodthirsty badgers, armed with rifles, are going to attack Toad Hall this very night, by way of the paddock. Six boatloads of Rats, with pistols and cutlasses, will come up the river and effect a landing in the garden; while a picked body of Toads, known as the Die-hards, or the Death-or-Glory Toads, will storm the orchard and carry everything before them, yelling for vengeance.

Putting the book down, Howie said, "Man, this sounds like it gets pretty intense. The cover says it's a children's book."

"You're reading ahead, Howie. Way ahead. Start at the beginning."

"Unlike Teddy, I may have a hard time accepting these kinds of characters as old friends," Howie said. "I think I'll just watch the scenery. I may be in over my head with this one."

Bud grinned as Howie tossed the book onto the back seat next to Lindie. She startled, then went back to sleep.

They eventually passed the Mother and Daughter, two tall spires, one smaller than the other, which were technically the end of the Teapot Canyon crossing. Now they passed the Wall, a tall long rock form with a fitting name, signaling the beginning of the Land of Standing Rocks.

Bud knew all these monoliths and walls were made of the Dewey Bridge Formation, for his geologist friend Shorty had pointed similar forms out to him in Arches National Park, saying the rippled rock was thought to have been caused by the impact from the huge meteor that created Upheaval Dome in Canyonlands.

They rode along in silence, then Howie asked, "Did you really think my song was OK, Sheriff? It was kind of hard to read those guys last night. I don't know if they liked it or were just being nice, except Eldon, of course, 'cause I know he didn't like it."

"Well," Bud replied. "You know Eldon can be a bit crotchety. He won't admit when he likes stuff. It hurts his image. But I thought it was great. It'll be perfect for your next concert."

"Thanks, Bud," Howie replied. "But do you really think we're going to find any clues out here as to what happened to that oboe player? Do you think he was murdered?"

"The jury's out on that one, Howie, but I think so. We'll see what the autopsy report says."

"What if he had a heart attack, or maybe just fell off that cliff he was under?"

"Both are very possible," Bud answered. "But if he was murdered, we need to make sure we've covered every possible clue. Cynthia said there's a big storm coming in, and the Maze could very well be shut down for the winter. I have a feeling this is our last chance to check things out."

"That guy Tex, he's the one who called it in, right? The guy at the cafe?"

"Yes, he was there."

"Did you question him pretty thoroughly, Sheriff? He seems like he'd have some answers if he was there."

Bud paused, wondering if he had indeed thoroughly questioned Tex.

"I thought so, Howie, but maybe I need to talk to him some more. We were busy trying to retrieve the body."

In the distance stood the impressive Chocolate Drops, a series of dark forms high on the skyline. Next in view was Standing Rock, then Chimney Rock, the distant Needles across the Colorado River now visible.

Even though they were now in what the park called the Maze District, Bud knew the real Maze was immediately to their north, a vast network of canyons that all pretty much looked the same. It was an area with wondrous arches and colorful layercake walls that were generally unscalable. The Ancient Ones had left their mark in the form of rock art there, some of which was truly amazing, such as the Harvest Scene pictographs with their large anthropomorphs, one even dressed in stripes.

Bud had hiked down there years ago with a friend, and they'd nearly gotten lost, wandering for some time in the labyrinth of canyons until Bud finally recognized a twisted dead juniper they'd passed on the way down into the canyons.

It had been tricky climbing back up to it, and his friend had managed to get himself in a bit of a pickle, hanging onto a large cliffrose growing in a cleft in the rocks, until Bud had managed to scoot along a small shelf and help pull him up to safety.

And even though Bud had always had immense respect for the harshness of the canyon country, it had taught him that the Maze was a world all its own and not a place to take the gift of life for granted.

20

Howie had taken turns reading the book and staring at the scenery, and Bud had stopped several times to let Lindie out and take a break, pouring himself and Howie coffee from his thermos. They now began the gradual descent to the Dollhouse, the end of the road, which was now becoming more washed out and technical.

"What are we looking for out here, Sheriff?" Howie asked.

"I don't know. Anything that might be out of the norm. I want to measure the distance the body was from the cliff, that kind of thing."

"How can you do that without the body? And what would that show?"

"I left some rocks in place. I can do the measurements and figure out if he was maybe pushed or not by how far from the cliff his body landed, though it's iffy. Right now I'm just grasping at straws."

"So, you think he was up on the cliff and someone pushed him off?"

Bud replied, "I don't even know how he died without the report, Howie. He could've had a heart attack. But I just want to cover everything I can think of, since it's probably my only chance."

"And if he had a heart attack, all this is for nothing, right?"

"Not necessarily. We're getting to see some interesting country."

"But deep inside, do you think he was murdered?" Howie persisted.

"I try to stay neutral, Howie, so I'm not biased in my investigation. But I do have to remember what Andy told two different people—me and Tim—about hearing someone talking about getting rid of an oboe player."

"Maybe it was a cover and *Andy* did it, Sheriff."

"That has occurred to me. What the connection between the two would be isn't obvious at this point, though," Bud answered.

"Maybe he hates oboe music. Or it could be something from his childhood. Wasn't the oboe the duck in Prokofiev's *Peter and the Wolf*?"

"That's very helpful, Howie. When you figure it all out, let me know."

"Bud, the oboe can make lots of different sounds, and it can sound like a duck. It's kind of honky—hey, honky tonky. I could write a song about a honky tonk duck!"

Bud laughed, then recalled Tex telling him he'd heard the weirdest sound, like a combination of a "crazed insane mountain lion and a mad duck devil." He'd somehow figured the fellow had been playing his oboe, which was in itself odd, given it was dark and he was out in the wilds.

He then remembered Tex saying there were some duck petroglyphs nearby. They were now nearing the hoodoos of the Doll House, and he said, "After we look around, let's see if we can find some petroglyphs. Tex said there were some nearby."

Bud parked as close as possible to the cliff where they'd found the body, then got out, leaving Lindie in the FJ with the windows partway down.

"I don't want her potentially messing up tracks or anything," he explained. "I'll let her out when we're done."

They walked over to where Bud had carefully placed a few rocks to outline where the body had been, and pulling out a measuring tape and notebook, they began measuring the distance to the cliff base. They then walked around looking for footprints or any kind of clue as to what had happened, but found nothing. Next, they climbed up the back of the cliff above the body's resting place.

"Look over here, Sheriff," Howie said, calling Bud to the edge of the cliff. "There's scuff marks like someone was wrestling around or something."

Sure enough, Bud noted that the dirt had been scuffed up, though he wasn't able to make out individual tracks.

"Do you think it's from the oboe guy, or maybe just some animal bedding down or something?" Howie asked.

"I don't think an animal would bed down here, Howie," Bud replied. "It's too exposed. My gut's saying this is human-made. Let's backtrack and see if we can find any tracks leading up here, though it's going to be difficult, with all this slickrock."

The pair carefully walked in a grid pattern, looking for tracks, until Howie said, "Eureka! Over here!"

Bud walked over to where Howie pointed to a long narrow track leading back down the back side of the escarpment. He took photos with his pocket camera, putting a quarter next to the track for scale. He then zoomed in to capture the tread pattern.

"Someone came up here with a dirt bike, Howie," he said grimly.

"Could it have been the oboe player?" Howie asked.

"Possibly," Bud answered. "But it's not very probable. If the oboe player came in by raft, as I'm pretty sure he must have, then the odds of him having a dirt bike are slim to none."

"Maybe someone came in later, after you guys retrieved the body," Howie said.

"Maybe, but the tread looks about the right age for when we found the body."

"How can you tell?"

"When we were down measuring how far the body was from the cliff, I checked out the amount of degradation of our tracks when we were here before. It's hard to explain—it's the kind of thing you get better at the more you practice. But this dirt-bike track looks like it has about the same amount of degradation."

"You check out the edges of the tracks and all that?" Howie asked.

"Yes, and the baseline of the ground, as tracks will change that, and you look to see how close the ground is to returning to its baseline. If the ground was smooth, a track will often rough it up, and if was rough, a track will smooth it out. But it will eventually even out to where it started."

Now Bud paused, looking again at where the track went back down the back of the cliff. Spotting another track, he bent down to examine it, then took photos.

"Mountain lion tracks, Howie, and it was a big one."

"It came in after the dirt bike did, Sheriff. See here where it's on top of the bike track? I wonder if it wasn't watching you guys while you were out here getting the body. Spooky. Do you think it had anything to do with the oboe player's death?"

"I don't know, Howie, but we have no evidence yet that the oboe player was even up here. We haven't seen anything made by humans except the dirt-bike tracks."

Just then, they could hear something in the distance. Bud and Howie stood silent for a moment, then Howie said, "Lindie! She's barking at something, Bud!"

"That's her 'I'm defending my territory bark,'" Howie, and she sounds pretty serious. Let's get back down there!"

21

By the time Bud and Howie had made it back to the FJ, Lindie had stopped barking and seemed calm. Bud let her out, then began looking for tracks in the dirt near the vehicle, but found only his and Howie's.

"Would she bark like that at an animal?" Howie asked.

"Maybe, but not usually. I'm pretty sure someone came by, but they apparently didn't approach the FJ, probably because she was barking. Good dog, Lindie."

"She saved your thermos of coffee," Howie joked.

Bud replied, "That's about the only thing in there, except all our sleeping bags and tents and stuff—oh, and your guitar. If someone were to steal all that, we'd have to drive out instead of spending the night."

"What a disaster," Howie said sarcastically.

"I forget you don't like camping. How was last night in the RV? Any better than usual?"

"It was actually pretty comfy," Howie replied. "Except the cab window was open, and I could hear Phil talking to himself there in the front. It was actually kind of bizarre. I think he had a small recorder and was talking into it, taking notes."

"What was he saying?"

Howie replied, "Well, he was recording our answers to all the questions he'd asked earlier, mostly stuff like what was our favorite brand of hotdogs, what we put on them, why nobody had brought hot chocolate or smores, stuff like that. Then he went into more general stuff, like when he asked what we thought about the future."

"I wonder what he's up to," Bud replied.

Howie continued. "He was becoming a pest earlier until Eldon pretty much shut him down. It *was* getting pretty irritating. It was like he was taking a survey or something. I finally got up and closed the window so I could sleep."

"That's the same kind of thing he's been doing all over town," Bud said.

"Maybe he's from another planet and trying to figure humans out. I say good luck with that one, if he is."

"Agreed. But let's fan out and see if we can find any tracks. Someone had to have come by," Bud said.

They began searching for tracks, the giant doll-like hoodoos towering over them, now casting enough shadow that it was becoming difficult to make out much detail on the ground beneath them. Finally, Howie yelled, "Sheriff! Over here!"

Bud and Lindie quickly went over to where Howie stood in a wide fissure between two hoodoos, pointing at tracks.

"These look old," Howie said. "But over here on the edge are more, and they're really fresh."

Bud could see where a set of older tracks went into the shadowy cleft, while another newer set followed.

He said quietly, "Howie, I think someone may still be back in there. No tracks are coming out."

"Maybe we'd better not follow them, then," Howie whispered.

Bud hesitated, then said, "You stay out here and keep watch in case someone comes by. Are you armed?"

"No."

"Well, then, keep Lindie with you on her leash. You can go sit in the FJ if you want. Here's the keys, but don't leave without me."

Bud handed Howie the keys.

"I would never do that, Bud," Howie said, handing the keys back. "In fact, I'm going in there with you. You have enough gun power for the two of us. I'll just follow you."

Bud unlatched the shoulder case holding his Ruger, then they slowly entered the deep cleft, sandstone hoodoos towering on each side of them.

It was dark enough that he had to strain to see, but he knew he could rely on Lindie to tell him if someone was near, and his eyes soon acclimated to where he could see better. They all crept along stealthily until the fissure began to widen to where the sun could enter. Now Bud could see that the cleft continued out the other side, opening back up. He sighed, knowing that whoever had been there ahead of them had probably gone on through.

They stopped, and Howie asked, "What's the big attraction in here?"

"I don't know, Howie," Bud replied. "Maybe we're all just following each other's tracks."

"Do you think it's maybe just some hikers or something? It is kind of fun walking between these sandstone giants."

"Could be, but it's late in the season, and Cynthia said there was nobody else out here, at least not anyone with permits."

Howie said excitedly, "Look up, Sheriff. I think this is why people are coming in here. It's those ducks you wanted to see."

Bud craned his neck back. There, a good 10 feet above them, was a petroglyph panel with a series of what looked exactly like ducks, each smaller than the first, which was around four feet tall, until the last was maybe a mere foot, if even that. They were connected by a single line that went through the middle of each. He counted eight.

"They have their ducks in a row, for sure," Howie mused. "I wonder what they signify. It's kind of like a convoy. Are they pictographs or petroglyphs?"

Bud thought of the trucker, Rubber Duck, in the convoy song, then said, "They're petroglyphs. See how they're incised into the rock? Pictographs are painted using plant and mineral dyes, like pictures. You can be safe and just call it rock art when you don't know which it is. But maybe they just signify plain old ducks. I believe this is Barrier Canyon style made by the Late Archaic people from possibly 2,000 years ago, maybe even farther back than that. They were nomadic hunter-gatherers."

"How do you know all this?" Howie asked.

"Wilma Jean and I have spent a lot of time in the museum in Price. This style is pretty distinctive—plus I've seen it in a lot of the canyons around this country."

They stood for awhile in quiet admiration of an artist who could create something that would last several thousand years or more out in the elements, using nothing but the horn of a deer or bighorn sheep and a rock to pound it with.

From nowhere, Howie said, "Bud, give me a leg up here."

Bud walked over to where Howie stood, then cupped his hands together to make a stirrup, hoisting Howie up, who then put his other foot in a small indentation in the rock wall and pulled himself upwards even farther.

"Bingo!" Howie said, quickly sliding back down, holding something long and black.

"What is it?" Bud asked. "How did you know it was up there?"

Howie pointed to a small pile of rock rubble. "That looked like someone had cleaned the rubble from a nook in the sandstone, and I wondered if it wasn't to hide something. And Bud, this sure isn't several thousand years old."

Howie held up what looked to be a hard vinyl black instrument case with the word "Yamaha" stamped on it in gold.

"I'll be darned," Bud whistled. "I bet an oboe would fit perfectly in that. Good sleuthing, Deputy—I mean Mayor."

"Help me back up. I want to make sure there's nothing else up there," Howie said.

He was soon back down, empty-handed. "Nope. Nada. Sheriff, sometimes I wish I was still your deputy. This mayor thing kind of mystifies me as to what I'm supposed to do. But I have a feeling the tracks we followed weren't just in here to look at a bunch of ducks. Maybe we should head back to the FJ."

With that, they turned to go, returning as fast as possible to Bud's FJ, all the while looking over their shoulders.

22

Bud and Howie sat in the front of the FJ, Lindie in the back, the oboe case between them, wrapped in a plastic bag from the Melon Harvest Grocery to preserve any fingerprints. The sun was beginning to set, and they knew they needed to get camp set up soon or it would be dark and they'd be doing it in the FJ's headlights.

Howie asked, "Should we open the case, Sheriff? It might have something important in it. Why else would somebody hide it like that?"

"I'm debating on that, Howie," Bud replied, taking some Life Savers from his pocket and offering Howie one. "It might be better to do it in a controlled environment."

Howie asked, "Do you think it might be full of red ants or something? Maybe harvester ants? Do they have those around here?"

"I don't even know what harvester ants are," Bud replied.

"They call them that because they collect seeds and stuff. They build really big nests and are red like fire ants. They have them in arid places. My dad was up in the Bighorn Basin in Wyoming once, and he said they're all over up there. You can even see their mounds on aerial photographs. They really hurt when they bite because they reach up and sting you with this stinger on their abdomens while they're still biting you with their pinchers."

"I don't know, Howie, but now I'm going to be itching all night. I'm thinking we might not want to camp here, even though Cynthia assigned us this site."

"Agreed," Howie said. "I'd personally like to head on home. I about froze last night. It's getting too cold to camp. I couldn't get the heater in the RV to work."

"We won't have time to get out before sunset, Howie, and there's no way I'm going to try the Golden Stairs in the dark. But let's head on up the road. We could maybe camp over by the Standing Rock or someplace not very close to here. I think Cynthia would do the same, given there may be someone about."

"Let's drive to the bottom of the Golden Stairs, hike up, get the heater going in my RV, then hike back down in the morning and drive out," Howie suggested, his face lighting up.

"By the time we got there it would be way past dark, and hiking two miles up a steep shelf road in the dark isn't very appealing," Bud replied.

Howie said, "We'd better get going, then. Golden Stairs it is."

Just then, they both jumped as Lindie started growling at someone tapping on the window. It took Bud a minute to make out who it was in the fading light, then, seeing it was Andy, he rolled his window down.

"Evening, Andy," he said. "I figured you'd be down the river by now with your compadres."

"Evening, Sheriff," Andy replied, saluting him, then, seeing Howie, added, "Evening. Nice jacket."

Andy sighed, then said, "I should be with the expedition, but they've gone missin'. Hae ye seen anything of 'em? What are ye doin' up here agin? No boat this time, eh?"

"We're in this contraption called a vehicle, Andy," Bud replied. "In case you were wondering what it is. And Howie's jacket, those are called rhinestones."

Andy looked slightly irritated, then said, "I know what a vehicle is, as well as rhinestones, though I have no idea why he'd be wearing such. Did you come to see the ducks?"

Bud noted he'd suddenly lost his Scottish accent.

"We did," he replied. "Did you see them, too?"

Andy said, "I was in there and thought I heard talking, so I came back out. I'm camped back there in the rocks. Seems safer."

"Safer from what?" Howie asked.

"Mountain lions. I've seen several up here. Back in there I have rocks on three sides."

Howie replied, "It was probably the same one. Lions are territorial."

Andy, ignoring him, was now pleading."Are you going back out? Can I go with you?"

Bud, wondering what was going on, asked, "You say your friends are missing? How do you know?"

Andy replied, "I've been staying down at the beach, sleeping in my boat, waiting for them to come by, but I decided to hike back up here and see if anyone was around. Then I went back over to the edge of the cliff and saw the other dories down below, but there was nobody around. I have no idea where everyone went. If they came up here, I'd have crossed paths with them, as there's only the one trail up. They've just disappeared. I don't want to go back down there. All those empty boats remind me of the Flying Dutchman."

Bud now smelled alcohol, then noted Andy held a small flask down along his side, as if trying to hide it.

"Gave up on the Life Savers, eh?" Bud nodded at the flask.

"I ran out. Those things are addictive. I can still taste the pepper-mint, I ate so many. I just happened to find this little bit o'whisky in one of the boats. It's helpin' me get over me fear of lions."

Bud noted that the Scottish accent was back.

"Better not get over your fear too much if there's one hanging around," Howie said.

"Are you fellas going out or not?" Andy asked.

"We were going on up the road to camp, but maybe we'll stay here instead," Bud answered, nodding to Howie. "That way you can go sleep in your camp and we can meet here in the morning and head out together."

"Would you happen to have anything to eat?" Andy asked. "And say, did you find anything unusual back there by the ducks?"

"We're going to set up camp and then make some dinner," Bud replied. "You're welcome to join us. But what kind of something back there? What are you talking about exactly?"

"Never mind," Andy replied. "I'll head to my little camp in the rocks and freshen up a bit, then join you for dinner. The Major always said we should freshen up before dinner."

"The Major?" Bud asked.

"You know, Major Paul."

Bud shook his head as Andy disappeared back into the hoodoos.

"Freshen up his palette with some whiskey is what he meant, Bud," Howie remarked. "And who's Major Paul? I take it we're staying here instead of going back up the road?"

"Sorry, Howie, but the idea of him riding with us while he's all schnockered up makes me want to wait until morning, when he'll hopefully be sober. And knowing it was him who came by the FJ takes away some of that hesitancy I had, wondering who was out and about. Plus, his buddies may show up, then he could go out with them instead of with us. It's a win-win all around."

Howie thought for a moment, then asked, "Is schnockered a real word?"

Bud laughed. "I used it and you understood it, so it must be. But let's get camp set up and make something to eat. And Lindie needs her dinner."

He took a can of dog food from the FJ and opened it, feeding it to her with a plastic spoon.

"She's pretty civilized," Howie remarked.

"I forgot her bowl," Bud replied.

Andy was soon back, waiting for dinner like a hungry coyote. Bud opened a can of pork-and-beans along with some canned corn and Vienna sausages, then threw them all together in a pan and warmed them on his one-burner Coleman stove. For dessert, they each had slices of an apple pie Wilma Jean had sent along.

"That was the best meal I've ever had," Andy declared, the alcohol obviously settling in.

"Can you make it back to your camp alone, or do you need help?" Howie asked.

"I'm a shtubborn Scotsman," Andy replied. "We're genetically predishposed to being able to drink whishky all day. I'll be fine."

With that, he stumbled off, Bud and Howie watching to make sure he headed in the right direction.

It was soon dark, and Bud sat in silence, marveling at the night sky, feeling a little edgy knowing there might be a mountain lion around. He wanted to build a fire, but knew it was prohibited in the national park. Howie seemed unperturbed by it all, sitting on the ground and leaning against the FJ, reading *The Wind in the Willows* by headlamp.

Finally, he said to Bud, "Listen to this. The Water Rat's talking to some swallows who are getting ready to go south. He's trying to persuade them to stay. The swallow is trying to explain how migration works.

> *You don't understand, naturally. First, we feel it stirring within us, a sweet unrest; then back come the recollections one by one, like homing pigeons. They flutter through our dreams at night, they fly with us in our wheelings and circlings by day. We hunger to inquire of each other, to compare notes and assure ourselves that it was all really true, as one by one the scents and sounds and names of long-forgotten places come gradually back and beckon to us.*

Howie turned his headlamp off and sat, silent.

Finally, Bud said, "You know, that describes exactly how I feel about this country. It seems kind of wild sometimes, and I look forward to the security and safety of home, but it always calls me back, beckons."

"I say I don't like camping, Bud, but being out like this could really grow on a person. I'm starting to see why you like it so much—minus drunk Scotsmen and mountain lions, that is."

"Well, now that you have an RV, you and Maureen and the little guy can get out anytime you want," Bud replied. "But I'm gonna hit the hay. G'night."

As Bud crawled into his tent, Lindie by his side, he could see that Howie had turned his headamp back on and was again reading.

Bud zipped up the tent door, slid down into his bag, pulled Lindie's bag up around her, then quickly dozed off, dreaming he was a swallow on his way to Mission San Juan Capistrano, wherever exactly that might be.

23

Bud woke, thinking it was morning, surprised when he unzipped the tent door and could see it was still dark. Orion hung in the night sky with the stars of Gemini—Castor and Pollux—twinkling brightly, while the Dog Star, Sirius, watched over all, guarding them from falling stars.

Zipping the tent back up and wondering what had awakened him, he then heard it again—someone was talking in the distance. Were Andy's friends in the neighborhood?

Slipping into his clothes, he grabbed his jacket and headlamp, put Lindie's leash on her, again unzipped the tent, then stumbled into the night. He had no intention of seeking out whoever was the source of the sound, especially if it was the Major and his pirate bunch, but he wanted to know more about what was going on.

Leaning on the FJ and listening, he could tell it was coming from over by the hoodoos where Andy's camp was located. Had his friends found him? He hoped so, for that would mean Andy wouldn't be riding out with him and Howie, though he wasn't sure he wanted to meet the bunch close up, given their seeming roughness.

After awhile, he decided it was just one voice. He turned on his headlamp and led Lindie over to the hoodoos, walking between them into the passageway that held the duck petroglyphs. It felt spooky, the way the cleft tightened, and he almost backed out, thinking that whatever it was could wait until morning. But it was Andy's voice, and he sounded troubled, so Bud carried on.

He finally got to where the passageway opened back up, the voice now loud enough to easily understand, just around the corner. Bud turned his light off and stood in silence, listening.

It was definitely Andy, and instead of talking loud like he had been, he was now muttering to himself. Bud strained to listen.

"I didn't mean to kill him," he said. "It was self-defense. I didn't mean to. I'm not the kind of guy that kills people."

Bud could tell Andy was now full-on drunk. He must've finished the flask, Bud mused. He now muttered something that Bud couldn't make out, then, becoming agitated, began talking louder and louder.

"If that dang dog had just gone its own way. It didn't have to come after me like that. I wasn't doing nothin'. That was self-defense, too."

Now it sounded like Andy was crying. "Seems like everybody's got it in for me, especially the Major. I wish I'd just stayed home."

Andy was now full-on sobbing, then, seeming to regain control, said, "Oh well, at least I know they'll find me innocent. But I hate trials like I hate wormy bacon. You never know if it'll kill you or not until you're already dead. And where the heck is that dang oboe case?"

Bud now heard a soft thud, then everything went quiet. He turned his light back on and went around the corner, where he found Andy crumpled into a heap, either unconscious or asleep.

Shining the light around, he found Andy's sleeping bag laid out on the sand, and next to it was the flask, now empty.

It was getting cold, and Bud knew he couldn't just leave Andy on the ground, so he grabbed the sleeping bag and threw it over his shoulder, then tried to coax Andy awake. Andy mumbled something, then passed back out, and Bud finally managed to get him on his feet enough to half-drag him back out from the hoodoos to where the FJ was parked. As sheriff, he'd had to deal with more than one drunk, and he was adept at it, though it was a skill he wished he didn't need.

Finally settling Andy into the sleeping bag, which he'd put next to the FJ, Bud crawled back into his tent, Lindie by his side. He lay there awhile, unable to go back to sleep, listening to Andy's soft snoring, wondering if he had enough evidence to arrest him.

Had he heard Andy just confess to killing the oboe player? If not, who else could it be? In any case, it appeared that Andy had indeed killed someone, yet how did he know he was going to be found innocent through self-defense? And had the oboe player somehow had a dog along? If so, what had happened to it? And had Andy been the one to hide the oboe case up in the hoodoo wall?

Unable to sleep, Bud tossed and turned until he could no longer hear Andy snoring. He finally slipped into a light sleep, awakening every few hours until he finally gave up and got up, slipping from his tent, Lindie at his heels.

It was chilly, and he could see frost on the FJ's hood. Firing up the little stove, he boiled water, then dumped in some coffee grounds, let it simmer for a minute, then poured it into his cup, adding some half-frozen canned milk.

Even though a hint of dawn was now appearing over the eastern horizon, it was still cold, so he got into the FJ, Lindie jumping into the back. He sat for awhile, sipping the hot brew, finally warming up.

The bag with the oboe case sat where he'd left it, down near the gear shift, and he suddenly felt the urge to see what was in it. He knew Howie would want to be there when he opened it, but what if it did contain something dangerous? Wouldn't it be better if he opened it alone? And what about Lindie in the back seat?

Feeling like he was overthinking the danger, he slipped on his gloves then picked up the bag and took the case out, flipping the two gold clasps open.

Slowly opening the case, he saw nothing inside except a piece of rolled-up paper held with a paper clip.

Removing the clip, he carefully unrolled the paper, squinting to see. Finally taking his flashlight from his pocket, he could make out some kind of sheet music, completely handwritten in a dramatic flourish, including the staff and notes. It looked old, though the paper was standard office paper, and Bud knew it had to be a photocopy.

Along the top was the title: *Beethoven's Tenth Symphony*, and along the bottom, written in ink on the photocopy were the words: *SLC Airport. Locker 14, 23-22-16.*

Now something fell from beneath the velveteen liner of the case. Picking it up, Bud could see it was some kind of check. Holding it up to the flashlight, he could make out the amount of $235,000. It was made out to *Reece Billings/Chicago Symphony Orchestra* on the First Midwest Bank of Chicago and signed by George Picco.

Bud whistled softly, then replaced everything in the case as he'd found it, wrapping it back up in the grocery bag.

He had no idea what he was looking at, but he knew deep in his gut that Reece Billings had been murdered, and his death had something to do with what was in the case. He vowed, then and there, to figure it all out.

Slipping back out of the FJ, Lindie behind him, Bud quietly closed the door so as to not wake Howie or Andy. Walking around the FJ to where Andy was sleeping, Bud stepped softly. He wanted to check and make sure everything was OK. He had decided he should arrest Andy and take him back to Green River. If he was innocent, it would work itself out, but the previous night's confession seemed evidence enough.

To his surprise, there was nothing there, not even a sleeping bag.

It appeared that Andy had quietly flown the coop sometime during the night.

24

Bud and Howie stood on the rim above Spanish Bottom, surveying the beach below. Handing Howie his binoculars, Bud said, "I count four dories down there and zero people. See what you think."

After a few minutes, Howie said, "You know, if you fell off here, you'd starve to death before hitting bottom. But I don't see anyone down there, Sheriff, not even Andy."

"I wonder where he went off to?" Bud asked. "He wasn't back in the hoodoos, 'cause I looked right after I noticed he was gone. But he did go back in there to retrieve his flask."

"It's a mystery," Howie replied. "The Mystery of the Disappearing Lunatic. But he obviously can take care of himself, Bud. He's been on the river for some time now."

"As long as he doesn't find any more whiskey," Bud replied. "But I did find the leather notebook I saw him carrying when I first gave him a ride. He left it at his camp. It was all covered with sand except one corner."

"Did you look in it?"

"Not yet."

"What if he killed the oboe player and took notes?" Howie asked. "But can we go back now? I'm real worried about getting caught in that storm Cynthia mentioned. Did you notice the mares' tails coming in? And I froze again last night."

"You need a warmer bag," Bud replied. "But let's get going. I'm with you, we need to head out."

They were soon on the road back to the Golden Stairs, Bud half dreading the climb back out, though he knew it would be several hours before they reached them. There was a time he enjoyed roads like that, but he guessed he was getting older, as he now just felt they were more obstacles than challenges.

As it often is in such enterprises, it didn't seem like it took nearly as long to get back as it had to come in, and they finally found themselves at the base of the long switchbacks of the Golden Stairs. It was a slow climb, and he and Howie had to rearrange a few rocks, but they made it to the top.

The view down into Ernie's Country was just as stupendous as when they'd first stopped there, and Bud paused to scan the countryside with his binoculars. He examined the Mother and Child, far below, rubble spilling down their sides from erosion.

Finally, they drove to the spot where Howie's RV had been parked.

"This is where you parked it, right?" Bud asked.

"Yes, but where could it have gone to, Sheriff? Do you think it rolled off the rim?"

"Even if you'd left it in neutral, it couldn't have rolled that far. There's a bit of a hill between here and there, Howie. Let's see if we can find any tracks."

They got out of the FJ and looked around, and Howie said, "Somebody turned it around and took it back down the road toward Hite, Bud. How did they get it started?"

"Did you accidentally leave the keys somewhere obvious?" Bud asked.

Howie held the keys up. "They're right here in my pocket."

"These older vehicles are easy to hot wire—sometimes if you have the right-sized screwdriver that's all you need. And they knew how to jimmy the lock to get in. But who would steal a vehicle out here? It's unheard of."

"Someone tired of being on foot," Howie replied. "Would Andy be able to walk out this far during the night?"

"It's a long ways, not a distance someone could walk even in a long day, Howie. Besides, Andy was too drunk to walk anywhere, except maybe off a cliff."

Seeing the look of worry now on Howie's face, Bud added, "And we would've seen him if he had, 'cause we were right above the trail down to Spanish Bottom."

"Maybe he's out there somewhere lost, walking in a circle," Howie mused. "Sheriff, why do people always walk in circles when they get lost?"

"It's because some people have one leg slightly longer than the other, or if they are the same, one will be stronger than the other and you'll favor it."

"You're joking, right?"

Bud replied, "Try walking in a straight line with your eyes focused about five feet ahead of you sometime and see where you end up."

"I'd end up about five feet ahead of me," Howie replied. "But look here—more of those weird saucer-shaped tracks. That pod thing's been here."

Back in the FJ and on their way out, Bud said, "I'm wondering if that bunch on the river could've gotten up here and taken your RV, Howie. It would seem like something they would do. By the way, I opened the oboe case last night. I couldn't sleep."

"Was it empty? It felt pretty light."

"It had a photocopy of *Beethoven's Tenth* rolled up inside."

"The oboist must've been practicing it," Howie replied. "But since it's known as his *Unfinished Symphony*, it probably stops abruptly."

"He never finished it?" Bud asked.

"If he did, he didn't tell anyone," Howie replied. "It's pretty famous. It's part of the Curse of the Ninth."

"Never heard of it."

"You don't run in musical circles like I do, Sheriff," Howie grinned, then added, "And no need to mention me running in circles, Maureen already tells me that."

"But what's the curse?"

"It's this thing that classical musicians used to believe, that a composer's ninth symphony will be his last. He or she is fated to die while writing it or before completing a tenth. But I've always wondered if a composer could finish their tenth symphony without starting it and thereby get around the curse."

"How could you finish it without starting it?"

"Simple. You write the end first. You could call it *The Unbegun Symphony*—but I didn't make that up. PDQ Bach did."

"Who's PDQ Bach?"

"He's one of Bach's sons. He's still alive, I think."

"You're kidding, Howie."

"Actually, he was invented by a musician called Peter Schickele as a joke. Schickele composes parody under the name of PDQ. He's pretty funny."

"I think I've heard of him," Bud replied. "But is the Curse of the Ninth real?"

"Only if you're superstitious, Sheriff. It was touted by Gustav Mahler, who noticed a few of his colleagues had died after writing their ninth symphonies. For example, Beethoven, Schubert, Bruckner, and Dvorak had all died before or while writing their tenth symphonies. So Mahler figured out a way to beat the curse. He composed a piece that was a symphony in structure, but called it a song cycle. He then wrote his ninth, thinking he'd beaten the curse because the other piece was actually his ninth."

"Did it work?"

"He died of pneumonia while writing his tenth."

"Do people still believe in it?"

"Well, considering that a lot of composers didn't die after writing their ninth, the curse kind of went out of style. Joseph Haydn wrote over 100 symphonies."

"How do you know all this, Howie?"

"Sheriff, I'm the one who usually asks *you* that. But my mom was all into classical, and as you know, I'm into astronomy, and sometimes the two do meet. Did you know that the third largest crater on Mercury is named in honor of Beethoven, as is a main-belt asteroid?"

They were nearing the Hans Flat Ranger Station, and Bud could see there was no one there. Pulling over, he wrote a note saying they were out of the Maze and to watch for Howie's RV. He then stuck it in the iron ranger where one puts the money for their permits.

They now headed back toward the highway.

"It's late, but I'd like to stop at the Temple Mountain Cafe and get a taco, if you don't mind, Howie," Bud said. "Dinner last night kind of made me appreciate good food. Plus I want to see if anyone's seen your RV."

Howie replied, "That actually sounds really good. But Sheriff, I've been wondering, what do you think all these people talking about hearing music out in the canyons is about? Do you think the Chicago Symphony is out there? I mean..."

"Howie, we need to get in touch with that gal from Chicago who called you way back when and find out more. We should've done that days ago. I mean, if we have a symphony orchestra missing, well, we have something big on our hands. But I suspect it's all related to the fellows on that raft and the missing boatman, who Marty didn't seem to be too worried about. But I'll be darned how they could be in so many places—Red Canyon to Crack Canyon and all over the place."

"Maybe it has something to do with that gyrocopter."

Bud thought for awhile, then said, "Bingo. I think you may be onto something there, Deputy. But Howie, there was something else in that case—a check. A *big* check."

"How much?"

"Almost a quarter-million dollars."

Howie whistled, saying, "That's the kind of money people will kill for."

"Exactly," Bud replied, "And it had the combination to a locker at the Salt Lake Airport."

"They pay the money, then they get directions to the original manuscript. I wonder if it was stolen. But it doesn't make sense, Bud.

If whoever paid the money for the manuscript killed the oboe player, why didn't they take the case with their check and the directions in it?"

"Maybe the oboe player hid it, and they couldn't find it," Bud replied, "And if that's what happened, they'll be back out there looking, unless they're actually still there."

Bud now pulled onto the highway, the smooth surface feeling foreign after all the rough roads they'd been on. He drove north a few miles, then turned onto the Temple Mountain Road.

He was hungry and looking forward to a good meal at the cafe, but he wasn't looking forward to what else he suspected he might find.

He wanted to see if the tread on Hattie's dirt bike matched that of the tracks in the photos he'd taken.

25

Bud was in his office, happy to be there, especially given the way the wind was blowing, and he knew Cynthia's storm was well on its way. He'd carefully put the oboe case and Andy's leather notebook in the office safe.

He was still tired from their excursion into the Maze, and he'd seen neither hide nor hair of Howie and suspected he was home trying to catch up on all the sleep he'd missed from being too cold.

Bud had been busy since he got back, trying to line things up with his investigation as well as deal with the day-to-day things that went with being sheriff, things that had piled up while he'd been gone.

He'd had a message from Deputy Cal Murphy that the autopsy report was back, so he'd called, only to find Cal was out. Cal called back after a couple of hours, just when Bud was thinking about going to the Chow Down for some coffee and a doughnut.

"Emery County Sheriff's Office, Bud speaking."

"Bud, Cal here. The report says Reece Billings died from the fall he took. The medical examiner found no signs of foul play. He simply lost his balance and fell."

"He landed on his back, Cal. Did the coroner know that?"

"It's in the report we sent him. What difference does that make?"

"Well," Bud replied. "It depends on which way he was facing when he fell. If he'd been pushed from behind, he would've fallen on his face, as well as if he'd jumped. But landing on his back means he was maybe pushed from the front."

"He could've just stumbled and fallen backwards, Bud. Or twisted in a somersault while falling." Cal said. "No signs of foul play. It looks to be an accident, though there was another set of finger-prints on the oboe, but they didn't match anything in the FBI national database. I'm guessing he let someone else play it at one point."

"Cal, how many people walk around the tops of cliffs backwards?"

Cal was silent, then said, "I don't know, Bud. It seems like he was just some city fellow out in the backcountry, kind of ignorant of the dangers, and he fell. You can't make a case out of that."

Bud sighed. "Fax it on over, Cal, and thanks. Did anyone contact his next of kin?"

Cal replied, "I've been trying. His phone had his emergency contact name and number. I called the police in the town listed as their residence, but nobody's called back."

"Did you try the Chicago Symphony?"

"Yes, and no answer. Maybe something happened to the entire state of Illinois."

Bud replied, "We probably wouldn't hear about it out here for awhile if something had. But I'll see if I can get a contact number from Howie, as someone from the symphony called him not too long ago."

"They called Howie?"

"It's a long story, Cal. I can tell you later, but I have something I need to do right now. Send over that report and thanks again."

Bud stood, reaching into his pocket for a Life Saver, wondering if Reece had indeed just fallen or had been pushed. He panicked for a second, realizing his pocket was empty, then sighed. He'd just have to get another bag or two on his way to the Chow Down, no big deal, he thought, putting on his jacket.

Once at the store, he made his way to the candy isle, but couldn't locate the Life Savers. Finding Sherwyn, he asked, "Hey, Sher, where are the Life Savers?"

"Are you kidding me, Bud?" Sherwyn replied. "I've been sold out for days. Every time I get a new shipment, it's gone in a couple of hours. It's like a new fad or something. Everyone in town's asking for them."

"That's odd," Bud replied. "I wonder how they came to be so popular. Was there a special about them on TV or something?"

Sherwyn replied. "I don't know, but I can't get another shipment in for awhile."

Bud groaned. "Do you have anything similar?"

"Is this about that fiddling thing you've got going?" Sherwyn asked. "Why not try chewing tobacco?"

"Wilma Jean would have a fit," Bud replied. "You know I did used to smoke, Sher, though I wasn't all that dedicated to it. I mostly liked having something in my mouth to fiddle with."

"I know, I know," Sherwyn replied. "I was just kidding, though I could really make a fortune if everyone in town started chewing, the markup's so good."

"Your taxes going up would make up for it."

"How so?"

"Street cleaning."

"OK, how about cinnamon toothpicks?" Sherwyn asked.

"I don't think bakery stuff would work. I'd just eat it."

Sherwyn laughed. "No, Bud, not cinnamon *sticks*, *toothpicks*. You soak toothpicks in a vial of cinnamon oil and then chew on them. I sell them mostly to people who are trying to give up smoking."

"You sell the oil?"

"Sure. Let me get some for you."

Sherwyn returned from the back of the store with a box of toothpicks and a small vial containing what Bud assumed was cinnamon oil.

"Soak the toothpicks in the oil overnight, then you can put one in your mouth and chew on it. They last a long time. But don't soak them too long or they'll get really hot."

Bud grinned. Here was a habit that he could do on the sly, and it was much better than Life Savers, for they eventually dissolved and had to be replaced. He could suck on a cinnamon toothpick all day, and Wilma Jean wouldn't be the wiser, she'd just think he'd returned to the old toothpick habit he'd used to quit smoking.

Bud grabbed a couple of bags of red licorice, then went to the counter to have Sherwyn check him out.

"So, you're going to start a red licorice fad? Should I stock up on that?" Sherwyn asked.

Bud laughed. "No, Eileen Jensen brought me a candy jar full of red licorice the other day, and I put it on my desk for people stopping by. It was a big hit."

"So, I should stock up," Sherwyn said, handing Bud his change. "Be careful with that cinnamon. It can burn your mouth."

"I haven't had cinnamon toothpicks since I was a kid," Bud replied.

He walked back to his office, the wind picking up and starting to gust. He thought of Andy and his friends, wondering if they were still in the Maze, then of Cynthia and Gary, living out at Hans Flat. It seemed lonely and remote, yet free in its own way of all the impossibilities of civilization.

Just as he filled the candy jar, Howie walked in.

"Mind if I have some, Sheriff?" He asked, taking a piece of red licorice. "And what's that on your desk, if I might ask?"

"It's a vial of cinnamon oil to make cinnamon toothpicks, Howie. Are you all rested up?"

"Cinnamon toothpicks? Like the kind that were banned in school? And you've got them right here in the open, on your desk?"

"They're not illegal. Sherwyn thought they might help me with my fiddling."

"They *should* be illegal, Sheriff. Remember those kids who sold them during recess? Cinnamon stick pushers. They kept them wrapped in tinfoil, and we'd buy them for a nickel when the teacher wasn't looking. Man, the longer you chewed on them, the hotter they got. They were like a gateway drug, Sheriff."

"A gateway to what?" Bud asked, grinning.

"Atomic Fireball bubblegum."

"A real initiation into adulthood," Bud quipped.

Howie laughed, and taking another piece of licorice, stood. "I have to go see your wife."

"Where is she, anyway?" Bud asked.

"She's supposed to meet me at the bowling alley. I have some mayoral duties to attend to."

"At the bowling alley?"

"Yeah. She said we could have this week's rockabilly concert there, since it's going to storm, and I need to go set things up. People can get all hepped up on the music and strike out."

"Isn't that more of a baseball thing?"

"You know what I mean. I'm pretty excited to play my new song. See you later, Sheriff, and thanks for the licorice."

With that, Howie was gone, the wind slamming the door behind him.

Bud realized he'd forgotten all about going to the Chow Down for a doughnut and coffee, which had to be a first.

26

Bud had just downloaded the photos from his pocket camera, which included the pictures of Hattie's dirt-bike tires that he'd managed to get while Howie was ordering their tacos.

Just then, the phone rang.

"Emery County Sheriff's Office, Bud speaking," he answered.

"Is this the sheriff?" A woman's voice asked.

"It is," Bud replied. "Can I help you?"

"I'm wondering if something bad happened to the mayor. Is he still alive?"

Bud sat up straight. "As far as I know he is. Why do you ask?"

"I've been trying to get ahold of him for at least a week, well, for several days."

"He was just in here. Is there something I can help you with?"

"You could arrest him and handcuff him to his desk so I can catch up with him."

The woman started laughing, then introduced herself.

"I'm Katherine Chambers, communications and public relations liaison for the Chicago Symphony, but you can call me Kate."

"Nice to meet you, Kate. I'm Bud Shumway, Sheriff of Emery County. But before we continue, I have a question for you."

"Of course," she replied congenially.

"What's the difference between a symphony and a philharmonic orchestra?"

"I...I'm not really sure," she stumbled.

"When you called our mayor, you asked him that question, right?"

"Well, yes, I did. He said he knew the answer, but he never told me."

Bud laughed. "He thought you were asking a rhetorical question."

"No, I've been trying to get to the bottom of that for years. I've been told that philharmonic orchestras are formed by an organization of musicians, where a symphonic orchestra is formed and financed by a governmental entity. But in practice, I can't see any difference. They seem to be different names for the same thing—a full-sized orchestra of around 100 musicians, intended primarily for a symphonic repertoire."

"No difference, eh?" Bud asked.

"Well, I think the main thing is that these names are used to differentiate orchestras in the same city from one another, such as the London Philharmonic Orchestra and the London Symphony Orchestra."

"Well, thanks for the edification," Bud replied. "But I have one more question, then we can get to your business, I promise. See, it's not often that I get to talk with someone who knows about classical music—everyone around here's into rockabilly. But do you know anything about Beethoven's *Tenth Symphony*?"

"Beethoven didn't write a tenth," Kate replied.

Bud wasn't sure what to say. Hadn't the sheet music read *Beethoven's Tenth*? He was sure it had. And even though Howie had said it was unfinished, it appeared he'd at least written part of it.

"Are you sure?"

"I'm sure. Now, can you get a message to the mayor and have him call me back? The sooner the better."

"Go ahead."

"Tell him I'm getting desperate to hear back from the musicians we sent out your way. It's been awhile, and I haven't heard a word from anyone. Have you or anyone else seen them? Do you think they might have gone missing?"

"So, there really *is* a missing orchestra somewhere out here?" Bud asked.

"Well, it's not a *whole* orchestra, just a quintet. That means five in classical talk—a clarinet, a flute, a bassoon, a horn, and an oboe."

Bud thought back to what Howie had said about musicians carrying a tuba around on the raft. He asked, "Would that horn be a tuba?"

"No, a French horn."

"And an oboe," Bud repeated quietly.

"Yes, Reece Billings. He's the principal oboist for the orchestra," Katherine said.

"You know Reece?"

"Of course I know Reece. He's my brother. Is everything okay? I've been worried about him from the start. Everyone in the orchestra hates him, and they're always talking about how they'd be better off rid of him."

"They hated him?"

"Of course. It's nothing new," she replied.

"When did you last talk to him?" Bud asked.

"I don't know, over a week ago. He called to say that they'd arrived in Green River, but I haven't heard from him since."

"Are you his closest relative? The one on his phone contact list?"

Kate paused, then replied, "That sounds really ominous. Yes, I am. Did something happen to him?"

Bud remembered something he'd read in a police procedural manual that said the use of the telephone to make a death notification was callous and insensitive. Besides, hadn't Cal said he'd called the police in her area? Surely they would contact her soon.

Finally, he asked, "Can I get some personal information from you, such as your phone number and address?"

Kate gave him her address and phone number, then said, "The Chicago Symphony received a grant from a donor who lives part-time in your area who wants to bring music to those living in what we call a classical music desert. We can't, of course, send an entire orchestra, but we can send our quintet. The idea was for them to hire a raft and go down the river out there—what's it called, the Green?—and find a spot where they could easily bring people to listen to a concert in nature's amphitheater. It would be an experience—a scenic boat ride coupled with fantastic music, an aural and visual treasure one wouldn't soon forget."

"I can see why you do their public relations," Bud commented. "And would this be free, or would these lucky souls have to pay for it?"

"Oh, it would be free. Like I said, the anonymous donor is paying for everything."

"You guys realize it's almost winter out here—actually, will be winter after tomorrow when this storm hits."

"Yes, we know, we know all about winter—we live in Chicago, remember? But the concerts wouldn't be until next summer. This is a scouting trip. But I'm terribly worried about everyone. Is there anything you can do?"

"We can put out a missing persons bulletin, but if they're out in the desert, nobody's going to be finding them until after this storm, I'm sorry to say. But there are reports of people hearing music out there, and I'm not quite sure what to make of it. Is there any way you can share who this anonymous donor is and where he lives?"

"I'm not privy to that information, or I would share it. All I know is he lives part-time near someplace called Hanksville. But in any case, I've booked a flight into the town nearest you, which appears to be called Radium. I'll arrive tomorrow at 3:12 in the afternoon. I would like for your mayor to pick me up, and it would be nice to have your newspaper cover it, since it's going to be a big deal for the town."

"We don't have a newspaper," Bud said. "The closest thing is our postal carrier, Wanda, who covers everything in town, but it's all word of mouth."

"No newspaper? Do you have a website?"

"Not to my knowledge," Bud replied.

"How can I do media coverage with no media?" Kate moaned.

"Maybe we can get the high-school paper to come down," Bud replied.

They said goodbye, Bud somewhat relieved that he could at least tell her about her brother's death in person the next day, though it was going to be a hard row to hoe.

He'd get Howie to go pick her up, then maybe he could tell her about Reece after she'd made the rounds and met all the town's dignitaries, though he wasn't sure exactly who that would be. Maybe Sherwyn could have lunch with her.

Wait! He knew he'd forgotten someone, and that someone knew more about classical music, at least the opera side of it, than probably most anyone, having once been a dignitary, at least in the music world.

That would be Jay Landowska, who ran the Wandering One B&B. It would be a good place to put her up, too, Bud mused. Jay was from New York, and as a former opera star, he could talk shop with the best of them, because he once had *been* the best of them. And his B&B would provide her with the privacy she would need upon learning of her brother's death.

Making sure the wind didn't catch the door, Bud locked up and headed to the Chow Down.

27

Bud sat kicked back in his leather recliner, a phone book in his lap and his feet up on the chair's built-in footrest. Pierre slept on top of Bud's feet, his head on Bud's left foot and his rear end on the right foot. It appeared that the little wiener dog had finally discovered that sheepskin slippers served better as comfy pillows than as chewies.

"Better not roll over in your sleep, little guy," Bud whispered. "You might land down inside the chair, and then what would you do?"

Just then, Wilma Jean came into the room, wearing her white silk pajamas with her fluffy pink robe and slippers.

She asked, "Hon, why are you reading the phone book?"

"I'm trying to figure out who in town would qualify as a dignitary," Bud replied.

"Nobody, but why do you need to know?"

"We have a VIP with the Chicago Symphony arriving tomorrow."

"Bud, a dignitary is someone who's important because of their high rank or office, like a general or such. So, nobody in Green River, like I said."

"What about Howie? He's the mayor."

"I guess he qualifies. You're wanting someone to go meet this person?"

"Wouldn't you like to go see Peggy Sue down in Radium? You could pick up the symphony woman after you guys have lunch or something. She's coming in around 3. It's not everyone who gets to ride in a pink Lincoln."

"I thought you wanted a dignitary."

"You qualify. You own several businesses here."

"It would be more fun to pick her up in a pink Cessna."

"That would be great! Peggy Sue could pick you up for lunch at the airport, then you could meet this woman and fly her back here. It would impress the socks off her. She thinks we're a bunch of rubes."

"Some of us are, hon. But since when are you wanting to impress anyone?"

"I'm not, really, It's more for Howie and the sake of the town."

"Well, I forgot about this storm coming in. I may have to drive down there. Why is she coming here?"

"She's looking for a lost orchestra."

"What?"

"She can explain it better than I can. So you'll do it?"

"Only if Peggy Sue's available."

"Call her," Bud demanded as she walked back into the kitchen.

"It's too late. I'll call her in the morning."

She went into the kitchen, and Bud soon heard a whack. Lindie and Hoppie quickly hid behind his chair, Pierre still asleep.

Wilma Jean came into the room, carrying a rolled-up newspaper, and asked, "What's the lifespan of a house fly? I've been after this one for days."

"I don't know. Let me look it up." Bud took his laptop from the nearby coffee table, Pierre now waking as Bud gently let the footrest down.

"Sorry, little guy," he said, opening the computer and booting it up.

"Let's see. It says that the life expectancy of a housefly is generally 15 to 30 days, depending on temperature and living conditions. Flies dwelling in warm homes live longer than their counterparts in the wild."

Wilma Jean swung the newspaper again, whacking the window near Bud. All three dogs now ran for the bedroom.

"Wild flies? Well, this one lives no more. Finally! But I'm going to bed to read for awhile. This weather makes me want to get all snuggly and warm."

She headed for the bedroom, and since the dogs didn't return, Bud figured they'd all cozied up with her on the bed. He knew that earlier she'd gotten out the flannel sheets and down comforter for winter.

It felt too soon to go to bed, and besides, he figured he'd have to sleep at the foot now that the dogs had taken his place, so he instead keyed the search words *music manuscript* into the laptop.

Music manuscripts are handwritten sources of music. If the manuscript contains the composer's handwriting it is called an autograph. Music manuscripts can contain musical notation as well as texts and images.

This was interesting, but not very helpful, Bud thought. Maybe he should go to bed. He next keyed in the words *Beethoven manuscript.*

The complete collection of Beethoven manuscripts located at the Staatsbibliothek zu Berlin is available on microfiche.

This also wasn't very helpful. Maybe he should just wait until the symphony woman arrived tomorrow to ask about it.

He reached for one of the cinnamon toothpicks, deciding they'd soaked long enough. He didn't want them to burn his mouth, so he figured it was better to take them out sooner than later.

Chewing on one, he was surprised at the pleasant taste, which reminded him of snickerdoodles, which had cinnamon sprinkled on top. This made him think of Frosty, and he wondered when exactly the wedding was, and if he shouldn't be getting them a present, even though he hadn't yet been invited. Maybe Wilma Jean had something he could give them.

Now thinking of the oboe case, Bud searched on *Beethoven tenth symphony*.

When the composer died in 1827, he left his last symphony, which would have been his 10th, incomplete. Only a few handwritten sketches of this work have survived. Some are merely short, incomplete fragments.

So, Howie and Kate had been right. Beethoven had never finished his tenth symphony. But why had the photocopy looked like a real manuscript? Maybe he wasn't the one to judge, Bud mused, since he'd never even seen such a thing. Even when he hung out with Howie, he never saw any music, as Howie couldn't read music and just played by ear.

Now thinking more about the oboe case and the note reading *SLC Airport, Locker 14, 23-22-16*, he keyed in the words *Salt Lake City Airport locker*.

Luggage lockers or baggage storage facilities are not available at the Salt Lake City Airport. You should always check with the airlines for an early check-in or baggage drop options.

Bud was mystified. There was no manuscript, and there was no locker. It seemed both were as ephemeral as the music everyone had been hearing wafting through the canyons, though he figured that at least had a chance of being real.

He'd assumed George Picco had given the oboe player a check for the manuscript—or autograph, to be correct—of Beethoven's *Tenth Symphony*, and Reece had then left a note telling him where it could be found—in locker 14 at the Salt Lake City Airport—along with the combination.

Had Reece Billings scammed George Picco into thinking he had a very valuable work, then flown the coop, hiding the case with the check in it to retrieve later? Had George then caught up with him and killed him?

And who exactly was this fellow, George Picco? He knew Reece had to have known him, for his business card was in Reece's shirt pocket. And Picco had also visited the Temple Mountain Cafe, for Hattie had given Bud a pen he'd left.

Bud now pulled up the photos he'd downloaded before he'd gotten sidetracked. He found those he'd taken of the dirt-bike track out in the Maze, then loaded the photos of Hattie's bike's tread next to them.

Scanning both sets carefully, he could see they were a perfect match, down to the unique wearing of the knobby tires' edges.

Hattie's bike had definitely been driven to the cliff Reece had fallen from. The question now was, had Hattie been the driver? If so, what had she been doing out there, and what connection did she have with Reece, if any? She obviously knew Picco from the cafe.

Bud scratched his head, put his computer away, then noticed Wilma Jean had gone into the kitchen, the dogs at her heels. Looking out the window where the porch light was, he could see it had started to rain.

Wilma Jean returned with two cups, handing Bud one, then sat down across from him on the couch.

"What's this?" He asked.

"White hot chocolate," she replied. "Molly over at the B&B has this new recipe, and I just had to try it. It's half-and-half warmed up with white chocolate chips melted in, then you add salt and vanilla and put mini marshmallows and more white chocolate chips on top."

"It's delicious," Bud said, sipping the hot brew.

"It is, isn't it?" She replied, petting Hoppie, who'd managed to wiggle up beside her. "And very high calories. But hon, Sherwyn told me in the store this afternoon that cinnamon oil has been shown to restore hair in balding men."

"He just told you this out of the blue?" Bud asked.

"No, of course not, silly. I just asked if he'd seen you, and he said yes, you'd come in to buy some cinnamon oil. I asked what on Earth you'd want with that, and he told me about the hair."

"He was trying to cover for me," Bud replied. "I'm using it for toothpicks, and he thought I would want that kept confidential."

"Toothpicks?"

Bud groaned. "I guess the cat's out of the bag. It's my new fiddling device—cinnamon toothpicks."

"Well, see if it will help with the hair, Hon. I've noticed it's getting a bit thin in the back."

"That's just where my hat rubs," Bud said.

"Let's go to bed," she replied, standing. "This storm's coming in pretty fast. I hope the symphony woman's flight isn't cancelled. I'm not going to fly down there in this, so I'll drive."

"I hope the roads aren't bad," Bud replied.

He went into the kitchen, opening the back door to see how much rain was coming down. Even though it wasn't too bad yet, it was getting cold, and he knew there would probably be snow on the ground by morning, even though they never got much.

As he stood there, he thought again of Andy and his friends out in the Maze—had they had enough sense to come in out of the cold? Their dories would be frozen in before much longer, maybe even with this storm. And what were they doing out there in the first place? And who exactly was Major Paul, and why had his arm popped out? And why was Andy so adamant about staying in character, whatever that meant?

And was Hattie still out near Temple Mountain with her trailer? He knew she wanted to make as much money as she could, but it seemed to Bud it was time to bring it to the farm and make other plans.

He knew her family had been kind of a hardscrabble bunch, which had probably taught her to land on her feet, but he was glad Tex was there in case she needed help, as well as her ranger friend at Goblin Valley.

And what was Tex planning on doing for the winter? He'd mentioned going back home to his folks' place in Missoula, and if that was his plan, he'd better head out soon, though Bud knew he didn't have a vehicle. And should he consider him a suspect in Reece's death? Had he been thorough enough in talking to him?

And where was Howie's RV? He'd put out an APB on it, and

hoped it would be found soon. Howie had it insured and there really wasn't much in it, but Bud knew he'd put a lot into the decision to buy it and start camping, and he knew Maureen was disappointed. Fortunately, they hadn't spent a lot on it.

The wind pushed against the door, and Bud could see the rain was now indeed turning to sleet. He stepped back inside, tired, locked the door, and headed to bed, knowing it would seem even cozier than usual knowing it was cold and stormy outside.

28

Bud sat in his office watching it rain, drinking coffee and munching on snickerdoodle cookies. Mrs. Jensen had brought them by earlier that morning, along with a formal invite to her and Frosty's wedding, which would be in the park at the old square-dance bandstand, the same place where Eldon had held the wake for the good old days not long ago.

"And don't get all dressed up, Bud," she'd told him. "It's not going to be formal at all. In fact, Howie and his band are going to play afterwards. It's a potluck, so bring something tasty to eat."

Bud had never heard of a wedding potluck dinner, but it did sound like a good idea—maybe he could get Wilma Jean to make those enchiladas he liked so much.

"And no gifts," she'd added. "Me and Frosty have everything we need—unless you insist, then Frosty's really gotten fond of those Life Savers candies recently, so just bring a bag or two of those. I'll eat a few myself."

"That might be easier said than done," Bud had remarked. "Sherwyn says they're getting hard to keep in stock."

"That's 'cause Frosty's eating them all," she'd laughed.

"Will there be wedding cake?" Bud had asked hopefully.

"Of course! Your wife's making a big sheet cake. I'm sure it will be delicious."

Mrs. Jensen now gone, Bud was pondering the luck of having enchiladas and wedding cake in the same sitting. Jay, Howie, and Wilma Jean were all on their way to Radium in his wife's big pink Lincoln Continental to meet who Bud had started calling, in his mind, at least, Chicago Kate, as if she were some kind of gangster or something.

Howie hadn't wanted to go, saying he had important mayoral duties to tend to, but when Wilma Jean had pointed out that this was also an important mayoral duty, he'd given in. The trio was dressed to the nines, whatever that meant, and Bud hoped Kate would be dutifully impressed.

Bud booted up his computer and keyed in *dressed to the nines*.

This expression was originally used in the 18th century to indicate the highest standards and was simply "to the nines." The phrase is said to be Scots in origin, probably originally from "to the eyes" and meaning pleasant to look at.

Bud was pondering how much trivia there was in the world, just as the door opened and Phil Baker came in.

"Morning, Sheriff," Phil said. "You have time for a few questions?"

"Life sure is funny," Bud replied.

"What's that supposed to mean?" Phil asked.

"Nothing, nothing," Bud replied. "Just thinking about something."

"Which brings me to my first question," Phil said, sitting down. "What do you think about most of the time? Your wife, your job, money, politics, the future?"

Bud laughed. "I try not to think unless I have to. In fact, I can't think all that well without help."

"What do you mean?"

"I'm a fiddler. But Phil, I've been wondering, did you enjoy your trip out with the BOB-O's?"

"I did, except I'm supposed to be asking *you* questions."

"I wasn't aware of that," Bud replied.

"OK, here's this hypothetical situation. You're sheriff and..."

"But I *am* sheriff," Bud protested. "Are you putting together an encyclopedia of human behavior or something? You know, we had some Air Force guys visit us once pretending to be aliens to see how we would react—they were doing a sociological study."

"How did you react?"

"It wasn't a big deal to most of us. Are you doing something similar?"

"Well, no, but that's a good question to start asking people—how would you react to finding aliens among you?"

"The problem is, Phil, you probably wouldn't know if they were actually aliens or not. Kind of a Catch 20-20."

"You mean Catch 22—or are you talking about hindsight? But you ask what I'm doing, well, I'm here looking into the future."

Bud replied, "Well, that's different. It seems everyone else here is looking into the past." He thought of Andy, and added, "Some are even living the past for the first time."

"I don't understand."

"I actually don't either," Bud said.

"Anyway," Phil continued. "What do you think you could personally do to improve the future?"

"My own future or that of humanity in general?" Bud asked.

"Either way," Phil replied.

"I don't know. Maybe change my hairstyle or start a book club. Practice relentless self-improvement. Finish a *New York Times* Sunday crossword..."

Just then, his phone rang. Relieved, he answered, "Bud speaking, hang on a minute."

He offered Phil a cookie, said he had work to do, then showed him to the door, Phil looking frustrated.

Back at his desk, Bud asked, "Can I help you?"

It was Cal.

"Bud, I have someone here who says he needs to talk to you. He says the Canyonlands river rangers came down yesterday on their end-of-season patrol and towed everyone's boats back up here to Radium and put them in a warehouse, basically confiscating them for not having permits."

"Is his name Andy?" Bud asked.

"Yes, Andy Hall."

"Hall? That's the first I've heard his last name, Cal. He's part of that wild bunch going down the river. They've apparently disappeared. And I was getting ready to arrest him as a person of interest."

"He's sitting right here, Bud. He says you can help him. He came in here asking me to call you."

"Just arrest him and throw him in jail, then call me back, Cal. And ask him if he knows where Major Paul is."

"OK, but are you sure? What are the charges?"

"Murder. And he could use some decent clothes and a shower."

"Roger that. Hang on."

Bud could hear Cal talking to Andy in the background, then he came back on.

"He says he doesn't know anyone named Major Paul, but if you're talking about Major Pa-ool, he has no idea where he is."

"OK, Cal, lock 'im up."

"Roger."

Cal hung up, and Bud leaned back, trying to process what Andy had said. Major Pa-ool? He was sure he'd said Paul before, but with that weird half-Scots accent, who knew?

It had started raining again, and not wanting to go on patrol, Bud decided it might be time to take a look at Andy's diary, or whatever that big leather-bound book actually happened to be. He could check it out while waiting for Cal to call him back.

He got the book from the safe, turned up the heat a bit, kicked back in his chair, and promptly fell asleep.

29

Bud jerked awake as someone entered his office, silently seating themselves in the chair opposite his desk. It took him a moment to wake up to where he could see a rather short and somewhat stout fellow sitting in front of him, dressed in old-fashioned woolen pants and white long-sleeved cotton shirt with suspenders and tall worn leather boots. His left arm hung as if it had gone to sleep, and Bud could see that the sleeve was half-empty, a bit of straw sticking out.

"Afternoon," Bud said. "Have a snickerdoodle. Are you Major Pa-ool?"

Bud offered him the plate with the snickerdoodles as the man answered, "I guess maybe if you're from Louisiana. Just call me Major, or I guess you could call me Wes, if you prefer."

As the Major bent over to grab a cookie, Bud could see his left arm free itself from where it had been stuffed down inside his shirt.

Looking embarrassed and stuffing it back in, the Major said, "Dang arm! It would've been better to lose the whole darn thing. Instead I have to deal with trying to keep half an arm from showing. It's not easy. Keeps popping out."

The arm now back where it belonged, Bud asked, "What happened to your arm, if you don't mind me asking?"

"Better to ask than to wonder and keep staring at it," the Major replied. "I lost it at Shiloh. I was struck by a musket ball, and they had to amputate part."

Bud was shocked. "Seriously? Where was this?"

"Like I said, Shiloh."

"You mean the one in Tennessee?"

"Yes, during the Civil War."

"Our American Civil War? How is that possible? Was it a re-enactment or something?"

"Well, it happened, so it must be possible. I was made a lieutenant colonel afterwards, but I prefer to be called Major."

"Major Pa-ool."

"Whatever, Bod."

"That's Bud," Bud replied.

"You mispronounce my name, I mispronounce yours."

"I apologize, Wes. I'm glad to see you made it out of the canyons. But can I help you with something?"

"I'm wondering why you're arresting Andy. He didn't do anything. Yes, he's young and a bit naive, but he's good-hearted and means well, and he's a darn good cook, given what he has to work with, anyway—rancid bacon, dried apples, and mealy flour."

Bud wondered how the Major knew he'd had Andy arrested. He knew Cal would never tell anyone, and why hadn't Cal called him back like he'd wanted?

"Do you know Deputy Cal Murphy?" Bud asked.

"No."

Bud paused, not sure what to say. "What are you guys doing down on the river?"

"Everything—geologizing, geographizing, fossiking, botanizing, map-making. You name it. Trying not to get our lunch eaten, not that we have much lunch."

"Going where no man has boldly gone before, eh?" Bud asked.

The Major replied, "You mean going boldly where no man has gone before. Women have, though—Georgie White, for example. She was the first woman to run the Grand commercially, using multiple large army-surplus rafts lashed together. She was a legend, just like me, though I was there first."

Bud thought back to a display he'd seen at the River Museum. "She was also pretty infamous for being unsafe, if I recall. Didn't she have the distinction of having the first commercial river fatality on one of her trips, as well as the first helicopter rescue?"

"Well, as Mark Twain said, courage is resistance to fear and mastery of fear, not absence of fear."

Bud was confused. "I'm not following you."

"That's because I changed the subject," the Major replied. "I'm thinking again of Andy. He's a very brave fellow and exhibited raw courage in more than one example on this trip. He's not the kind of person who would kill someone. Cal made a false arrest."

Bud again wondered how he could possibly know that Cal had arrested Andy.

Bud replied, "But Andy admitted to killing someone. I was there when he said it. I heard him with my own ears."

"Yes, he might admit to it, but he didn't actually do it. You have the wrong person. You're blowing it."

"It wasn't Andy?" Bud asked.

"No."

"Hattie?"

"I don't know anyone with that name."

"Tex?"

"Ditto."

"George Picco?"

"Never heard of him."

"Maybe it was his fellow musicians and that's why they've all disappeared? They're on the run?"

"Preposterous! But you're not hearing what I'm saying. You're a good detective, you'll figure it out. Just remember that we don't have to be killed to die."

The Major reached over and grabbed another snickerdoodle, then opened the door and was gone, leaving a trail of straw behind.

Bud felt like he was in some kind of odd dream, and when the phone rang, waking him, he knew that was exactly what it had been.

Trying to shake off the strangeness, he answered, "Yell-ow."

"Bud? Cal here. I did like you wanted. You'd better have some good evidence to show that this guy belongs in jail. I still don't even think the guy at the Dollhouse was murdered. You must know something I don't."

"Cal, let him out on his own recognizance, then send him up here."

"I just put him in jail, for cryin' out loud. And his own recognizance for a murder suspect? Bud, we don't know anything about him. He appears to have no job, no family, no money, no car, no nothing, except a ticket from the park service."

"We'll let him out on the basis of abject poverty and being unable to go his bail. That's a legit reason."

"He has to put in writing he'll show in court, you know that's a requirement. But what's going on?"

"I'm having second thoughts, Cal. He may not have done it. I need to build a better case."

"You should've done that before I arrested him."

"I thought I had good evidence. He confessed to a murder, Cal. But Wilma Jean and Howie and Jay are down there. Did Peggy Sue meet up with them?"

"They're having lunch right now at the diner."

"Can you send this guy back up here with them?"

"You don't have a problem with a potential murderer riding in a car with your wife?"

"Not with Jay and Howie there," Bud replied. "This guy's actually pretty mild mannered. I think it'll be OK. Cal, I'm really having second thoughts on all this. Did he get some new clothes and a shower?"

"No. Well, yes, he's in jailbird clothes, but I have to reclaim those if I let him out and give him his old ones back, though they're basically rags. But OK, Bud. I'll call Peggy Sue and have her tell Wilma

Jean to come by the jail and pick him up, if you're sure that's what you want. Roger and over."

Now fully awake, Bud started another pot of coffee. He pondered awhile on his dream, looking to see if there really was any straw on the floor. Relieved at not finding any, he wondered what Chicago Kate was going to think of the motley crew coming to pick her up at the airport.

He couldn't help but smile.

30

Bud sipped a cup of hot coffee, wondering when Wilma Jean would arrive with Andy. He was starting to feel a tad anxious, not wanting to have to explain to Andy why he'd had Cal arrest him for murder. Chewing on a cinnamon toothpick, he finally picked up the phone and dialed his wife's number.

"Hi, Hon, we're almost back," she said.

"Oh, good, good," Bud replied. "But since I assume Kate is there with you, can you answer a question kind of surreptitiously?"

Wilma Jean answered, "I can try."

"Is she acting like she knows about her brother? Do you think the Chicago police told her yet?"

"Gosh, I don't think so, hon," she replied. "She seems like she's having a great time talking music with Jay, and Howie has a book he keeps reading quotes from."

"OK, I think I'll wait until tomorrow to tell her. Let her enjoy the day. Is Andy there?"

"He certainly is. He's riding here in the front with me. It seemed like the best place for him. He's actually sound asleep. Hon, am I supposed to bring him by your office? He thought I was taking him to the jail here, but I told him there wasn't one. He seemed upset."

"Listen, I'll explain later, but after you take Jay and Kate to the Wandering One B&B, take Andy over to the Melon View. Have Molly give him a room there, and tell him I'll pick him up after breakfast in the morning. Tell him he has to stay there."

Now his wife sounded put out. "I'm not sure what's going on here, Bud, but picking him up from the jail in Radium, and then him saying he's going to jail here, all with Kate listening, well, it's not such a good impression of our town, sweetie. Plus he looks like he was run over by a train—a train hauling pigs or coal—maybe both."

"Kate wasn't with you when you picked him up, was she?" Bud asked.

"Well, no, but she was there when he said you'd had him arrested for murder and that he was out on personal recognizance."

Bud wasn't sure what to say. Finally, he asked, "Could you take him to the second-hand store and buy him some clothes before taking him out to the Melon View? Tell him to take a shower."

"Look, Bud, is he someone that Kale and Molly should be dealing with?"

"He'll be fine. He's been on a river expedition and the park confiscated his boat for not having a permit. Like I said, I'll explain later. But hon, I'm not feeling too well. I'm taking the rest of the day off. I'm going to bed."

"The dogs will like that, but I hope you're not catching something. Can I get you anything?"

"Maybe some more of that white hot chocolate when you come home. But I'm going to just take it easy. Love you."

Bud hung up, called the State Patrol to tell them he was forwarding the phone over for the afternoon, then, carrying Andy's diary under his arm, locked up and headed for the bungalow.

Once home, he slipped into his Scooby Doo PJs and crawled into bed, the dogs beside him, happy to have him home.

He opened the leather-bound book, not sure what he was going to find. It did indeed appear to be some kind of journal, hand-written in a tidy print that he took to be Andy's. At the top of the first page was written: *Property of Andy Hall. If found, return to PO Box 1304, Rapid City, SD 57709.*

Bud noted that the words *Andy Hall* had been written over someone's else's name. Getting out of bed and going to the window where the light was better, he could barely make out *Andrew J. Frost.*

Back in bed, he opened the book to the middle and began reading.

> *August 10—We are three-quarters of a mile in the depths of the earth and the great river shrinks into insignificance, as it dashes its angry waves against the walls and cliffs, that rise to the world above; they are but puny ripples, and we but pigmies, running up and down the sands, or lost among the boulders.*
>
> *We have an unknown distance yet to run, an unknown river yet to explore. What falls there are, we know not; what rocks beset the channels, we know not; what walls rise over the river, we know not.*

Bud paused. He knew he'd read this somewhere before, it seemed so familiar. The writing, though dated, was fascinating. He continued.

> *August 13—We are now ready to start on our way down the Great Unknown. Our boats, tied to a common stake, chafe each other as they are tossed by the fretful river. They ride high and buoyant, for their loads are lighter than we could desire. We have but a month's rations remaining. The flour has been resifted through the mosquito-net sieve; the spoiled bacon has been dried and the worst of it boiled; the few pounds of dried apples have been spread in the sun and re-shrunken to their normal bulk.*
>
> *The sugar has all melted and gone on its way down the river. But we have a large sack of coffee. The lightening of the boats has this advantage; they will ride the waves better and we shall have but little to carry when we make a portage.*

Bud stopped, thinking about the dates. August? It was now November. Had they been on the river that long? Where and when had they started?

August 16—For years I have been contemplating this trip. To leave the exploration unfinished, to say that there is a part of the canyon which I cannot explore, having already nearly accomplished it, is more than I am willing to acknowledge and I determine to go on.

Bud flipped back to an earlier page in the diary.

July 6—We proceed, stage by stage, until we are nearly to the summit. Here, by making a spring, I gain a foothold in a little crevice, and grasp an angle of the rock overhead. I find I can get up no farther, and cannot step back, for I dare not let go with my hand, and cannot reach foothold below without. I call to Bradley for help. He finds a way by which he can get to the top of the rock over my head, but cannot reach me. Then he looks around for some stick or limb of a tree, but finds none. Then he suggests that he had better help me with the barometer case; but I fear I cannot hold on to it. The moment is critical. Standing on my toes, my muscles begin to tremble. It is sixty or eighty feet to the foot of the precipice. If I lose my hold I shall fall to the bottom, and then perhaps roll over the bench, and tumble still farther down the cliff. At this instant it occurs to Bradley to take off his drawers, which he does, and swings them down to me. I hug close to the rock, let go with my hand, seize the dangling legs, and, with his assistance, I am enabled to gain the top.

Bud paused, thinking. *Let go with my hand?* Does he only have one arm?

Now, as if a lightbulb had gone off, Bud suddenly sat straight up in bed, the dogs all sliding across the satin cover on the down comforter.

Of course! If it had been a snake it would've bit him! He *had* read this before—it was from the famous journals of scientist and explorer John Wesley Powell, first to go down the Colorado, back in 1869. This was the famous scene where he'd gotten himself stuck up on Echo Rock, which Bud knew was now called Steamboat Rock in Dinosaur National Monument.

He remembered this passage well, for it was very similar to what he and his friend had experienced when down in the Maze some time ago and Bud had saved his friend from falling.

It appeared that Andy had copied excerpts from Powell's journals, underlining and circling certain words and passages. And he'd been trying to say Powell, but with his fake Scottish accent, it had come out Paul, or Pa-ool.

Bud shook his head—it was all so obvious now. They were doing some kind of re-enactment of Powell's famous trip down the Green and the Colorado.

But who was Andrew J. Frost, the original name on the journal?

Bud slipped out of bed and went to get his laptop, grabbing a dish of vanilla-bean ice cream from the fridge on his way back.

Climbing back into bed and balancing the ice cream on one knee and the computer on the other, he keyed in the name *Andrew J. Frost*.

Finding nothing of interest, he next keyed in *Andy Hall*.

Andy Hall was born in Roxburghshire, Scotland in 1848 and emigrated to America in 1854 with his mother and siblings after the death of his father. His nickname as a child was Double Dare Dick, and he enjoyed adventure, joining a westbound wagon train at age 14. By 1868 he was in Green River, Wyoming, hauling wood for the Union Pacific.

It was there Major John Wesley Powell spotted Hall at the oars of a homemade boat and recruited him for his expedition. Hall wrote in a letter to his mother that he anticipated a long, wild journey that would be the greatest adventure in what had already been an exciting life.

On May 24, 1869, Powell, Hall and eight other men set off in wooden dories toward waters never traveled by Europeans. Powell wrote of Andy, "He is always ready for work or play and is a good hand at either. He can tell a good story, and is never encumbered by unnecessary scruples in giving to his narratives those embellishments which help make a story complete."

Hall eventually became a constable in Tucson. In 1879, Hall ate at a restaurant in Globe and was attacked by a dog as he left by the back door. Hall shot the dog, then crossed the street, then turning around, saw the dog's owner seemingly reaching for a gun in his pocket. The man made another suspicious move, and Hall shot him.

The court ruled the killing justified, as a gun was found beside the dead man.

In 1882, Hall was guarding a small mule train packing a $5,000 mine payroll when he was shot by robbers, who were later apprehended and hung.

Bud got up and, finding his phone, called the Radium County Sheriff's Department.

"Cal Murphy speaking."

"Cal, it's Bud. Drop the charges against Andy Hall."

There was a moment of silence, and Bud knew Cal was struggling with what to say.

"Alright, Bud."

"Andy Hall is no longer alive, Cal, so there's no way he could've killed anyone."

"I'm sorry to hear that, Bud. What happened?" Cal replied.

"No, no, he's been dead for a long time, Cal."

"Roger that," Cal replied, then added, "You need a vacation, Bud."

"Cal, I need you to do one more thing for me that could be very important. I need to head out to Temple Mountain, and could you run the name of one Andrew J. Frost in Rapid City and see what you come up with?"

"Will do, Bud, but you owe me lunch. Over and out."

31

Bud wasn't sure why he felt a sense of urgency about going out to the Temple Mountain Cafe, but he knew if he was going, he'd better get a move on, as the day wasn't getting any longer.

He hastily threw on his shoulder case and Ruger, then slipped into his warm plaid fleece jacket, grabbed some warm gloves, and quickly filled a thermos with coffee, adding a dollop of vanilla-bean ice cream, making what Wilma Jean called a Shumway Latte.

The dogs watched, knowing he was going somewhere, and after some indecision, he decided to leave them all, including Lindie, as he had no idea when he would be back, plus he was taking the Land Cruiser, which he seldom took the dogs in, seeing how it was the official sheriff's vehicle.

He left Wilma Jean a note saying he'd gone to Temple Mountain, then headed out the door, the dogs looking dejected. He turned and came back inside and gave them all Barkie Biscuits before heading out again.

Driving by the Melon Rind Cafe, he could see his wife's big pink Lincoln parked in front and knew they'd made it back and were probably all inside at that moment having pie and ice cream. He hesitated, wanting to stop and join them, the lights of the cafe looking especially welcoming in the grayness of the passing storm, but he continued on.

He was soon on the road to Hanksville, and as he drove along, he fell into that pensive mood travelers are prone to, when the mind, having nothing else to do, seems drawn to reminiscing and trying to figure life out.

He first wondered who Andy really was and where he was from, maybe Rapid City? And why did he seem so caught up in playing the role of someone long gone? It almost seemed as if he'd lost track of who he really was and adopted Andy Hall as his alter ego, which to Bud hinted at some kind of mental illness—or maybe he was just really into playing the role.

Was the bunch on the river doing a Powell re-enactment? Would Andy tell him if they were, now that Bud had figured things out, at least partway? Would Andy, or whoever he really was, now be more amenable to telling him what was going on? And where had they all gone to? Had they stolen Howie's RV and were maybe somewhere down at Hite in it? Bud knew the rig wouldn't have any problems going out that way, as it was a good road.

And speaking of people missing, where was the Chicago Symphony quintet? They had also just vanished without a trace, unless one counted the reports of mysterious music wafting from the canyons.

He now thought of Kate and knew she was part of the reason he'd taken the day off. He seldom had to tell people their loved ones were dead, and the thought of it made him want to go back to melon farming full-time. She would of course want to make arrangements for the body to be shipped back home, something Bud didn't envy.

Would there be yet more deaths to account for? Were the other members of the quintet besides the oboe player still alive? If so, what in hellsbells were they doing, and how were they staying alive, assuming they were still in the canyons?

Bud now thought about the dream he'd had about Major Powell and wondered if he'd dreamt about the real Major or the re-enactment Major. It would be quite the deal to have a conversation with the real Major, for Major Powell had been one of his childhood heroes, even though he knew it was just a dream.

He recalled reading the Major's two books, as well as the account of the journey by Fred Dellenbaugh, one of the other members of the expedition, and a warm feeling came over him.

He'd been in high school and was staying with his Aunt Rhoda and Uncle Chet there in Green River for his junior year. He'd holed up in their barn, sitting in the hay for hours, reading about Powell's expeditions, having checked the books out from the library. He'd been so caught up in the adventure that he'd vowed to become a river explorer when he got out of high school.

Of course, once he'd actually graduated, he'd gone on to other things, namely uranium mining, knowing that his inability to swim or even to float would be a difficult obstacle to a life on the river.

But he especially remembered reading a biography of the Major and how difficult it had been for him to lose his arm, as Powell had to relearn how to write and do things with his left hand, being right-handed.

He now recalled that the Major in his dream had his left sleeve stuffed with straw, and he knew it wasn't the real Major. For a moment, he felt disappointed, then he had to laugh at himself—after all, it was just a dream.

Or was it? He knew he must drive his subconscious crazy, ignoring its attempts to guide him along, making it resort to trying to get his attention through dreams. Sometimes he didn't even believe his subconscious existed, which he knew had to bother it enough that it was amazing it didn't give up on him entirely.

What exactly had the Major told him in his dream? He tried to remember, wishing he'd written it down, but he basically knew he'd told him he was barking up the wrong tree in suspecting Andy, which he now understood.

He'd mentioned Hattie and Tex and George Picco, but his subconscious had pretty much ignored him, saying it didn't know anyone by those names. Bud wondered why it would say that, since he'd met all but Picco, but he figured it must be talking rhetorically.

But what else had it said—he strained to remember, then it came to him.

You don't have to be killed to die.

Was Cal right, and the oboe player had died from his fall? But what if someone had pushed him? Bud reached for his thermos, holding it between his knees as he opened it, the Cruiser veering slightly as he poured coffee into the lid.

He would soon be at the Temple Mountain turnoff, and he still had no idea why he was going there. Maybe he needed to ask Tex more questions—and then there was the matter of Hattie's tire treads, or maybe he was just hungry for a taco.

He reached into his pocket for a Life Saver, then remembering he was out, wished he'd brought a cinnamon toothpick. For a moment, he felt panicked, but he then remembered a line about how someone had "the disconcerting habit of whistling when things go wrong."

He wasn't sure where he'd heard or read it—or was it maybe a line Howie had read to him from *The Wind in the Willows*? In any case, maybe he could appropriate the idea, even if it was just until he got home to the toothpicks.

He started to whistle aimlessly, then began to refine it into an actual tune. It was catchy, and he whistled a second verse. He was surprised at how easily it all came to him—maybe he could help Howie with his music, write the tunes while Howie wrote the words.

But when words started coming to him, he stopped whistling, paying better attention now, trying to think of what form of creative genius had just been freed in his brain.

Now turning onto the Temple Mountain Road, he began singing. It took a minute for him to realize what was going on, and he remembered that Wilma Jean had once told him that when he was trying to figure something out, there was no limit to the level of distraction he could attain, that someone could dismantle their house around him and he wouldn't notice.

This time, he'd been so distracted by thinking about everything going on that he'd thought he'd written an original song.

I'm risking my life on the highway of your love,
A hundred miles an hour and it ain't fast enough.

Bud laughed while continuing on down the Temple Mountain Road, whistling the tune.

He finally came to where the cafe should be, but there was nothing, not even a table or chair—in fact, all trace of a cafe having once been there had been blown away by the whistling wind.

32

Bud got out and walked around, at first unable to believe his eyes, but he finally decided Hattie and Tex had moved the trailer. It made sense, given winter was coming and there was no way to heat it, not to mention there would be virtually no traffic along the road.

But why hadn't Hattie brought it to the farm? She'd seemed grateful to Bud for the invite, and no one had called to tell him otherwise.

The place now looked desolate with its wide expanse of red desert sands pushing up against the white sandstone of the Reef. He knew it was because, like Frosty had kept reminding everyone, winter was coming—or was it because he'd wanted a taco? In any case, he felt stymied, thinking he wouldn't be having much luck that day in solving the oboe player's murder.

As he stood there, wishing he'd brought Lindie along, someone drove up next to him, and he turned to see it was Tex driving Hattie's pickup, its bed filled with chairs and tables and odds and ends from the cafe.

Tex got out, saying, "I thought that was you, Bud. You're probably wondering where the trailer went to, right?"

Bud grinned, saying, "I hadn't noticed until you mentioned it, Tex. How're you doing?"

Tex laughed, then said, "Hattie sold it. They came and got it this morning."

Bud was surprised, wondering where Hattie would now live. Her trailer was old and dented, and he knew she couldn't have gotten much for it. The aluminum needed polishing, and it also needed new tires.

"You wouldn't happen to have a taco in there, would you?" He asked, pointing to the old truck. "But where's Hattie?"

"She went for a ride on her dirt bike, since we'll be leaving tomorrow—one last desert ride. We're spending the night at her ranger friend's. She's been gone awhile. I'm supposed to meet her here."

"Where are you guys going?" Bud asked.

"Up to Price."

"Not to my farm, I guess," Bud replied. "But what's going on in Price? Is she going to reconnect with some of her family?"

"No, Bud, she's opening a cafe. Can you believe it? She's already talking to someone with a building to lease."

"That's great news, Tex," Bud replied, thinking she must've done pretty well on the trailer, or maybe someone was going to loan her some money. In either case, it was none of his business, though he wouldn't mind knowing.

"Bud, she sold it for a fortune."

"That's great, Tex. And what will *you* do?"

"I'm going to help her out. But Bud, she sold it for a fortune," Tex repeated.

Guessing he was supposed to ask, Bud asked, "How much?"

"It's a Bowlus Road Chief, and they only made a very limited number of them back in the 1930s. It was the world's first aluminum travel trailer. I guess Airstream copied the design, though they moved the door to the side. Hawley Bowlus sold only 80 Road Chiefs before returning to the aerospace industry to work for the war effort. Most of them are gone now."

"That's very interesting," Bud replied, wondering when Tex would tell him the important stuff, like what she got for it.

"Bud, I didn't know all this, but Hattie went down to her ranger friend's in Goblin Valley and looked it all up on the Internet. This was after she got an offer. She wanted to be sure she was educated about it. She had no idea it was worth anything. She told me she paid $600 for it."

"What did she get for it?" Bud asked again.

"It's a collector's item now, Bud. The last one on the market sold at auction for $187,000. She was offered $150,000 and she asked for $200k and George didn't bat an eye. It's already deposited in her bank account."

"Almost a quarter-million dollars?" Bud asked incredulously, thinking of another check for a similar amount sitting in the oboe case in his office.

"Yeah, I know. It's unbelievable. Anyone but George and one would think it was a scam."

"George bought it?" Bud asked. "Is he someone local?"

"He's kind of local. He lives part-time down by Hanksville. He saw the Bowlus every day when he was coming to the cafe for food, but I guess it took him awhile to really notice what it was."

"He was the same guy buying all kinds of food every day?"

"Yeah, our best customer, the one who pretty much kept us going, George Picco. I know him well. I stayed at his place for awhile. He's really wealthy, made his fortune in the aeronautical industry. When Hattie told me it was him, I wasn't surprised, as he's in love with anything to do with aircraft."

"But it's a trailer, not a plane," Bud pointed out.

"I know, but there's a connection. Hawley Bowlus, the guy who designed Hattie's trailer, was the Superintendent of Construction on Lindberg's Spirit of St. Louis. He actually gave Lindbergh flying lessons. He designed gliders and set a lot of records. I think that's part of why George was so interested in the trailer—it has a lot of meaning to him, him being all into aircraft history."

"And spending that much money wasn't prohibitive?"

"He dabbles in aircraft design for a hobby. He has an estate back in Illinois. He bought 600 acres out by Hanksville and put a modular on it, along with several hangers and an airstrip."

"He lives near Chicago?" Bud asked.

"Yes."

"Is he a classical music buff also?"

Tex laughed. "Oh yes, he would blast it away while we were working. He's especially fond of the Russians—Tchaikovsky, Rimsky-Korsakov, Mussorgsky, Rachmaninoff, Prokofiev, and Stravinsky, though Stravinsky later became an American citizen. But George also loved Beethoven."

"You sound like you know a lot about classical yourself," Bud commented. "But you worked for him?"

"I'm not into classical at all, but I'll never forget those names, since I heard their music every day. And yes, I did work for him, but when we finished the project, I needed a break, so that's when I headed out for the Maze."

Bud knew Tex had majored in structural engineering from when he and Cal had first met him out at the Dollhouse.

"You helped him with design work?"

"I did."

Bud continued. "And he's a classical music fan. Tex, would he be the kind of guy to collect classical stuff, like old manuscripts?" Bud asked.

"I don't know," Tex replied. "He does have that collector's mentality, though, so it's possible. He has the money to collect anything he wants."

Bud asked, "What kind of craft did you work on? Is it like a weird pod on chicken legs with saucer feet?"

Tex laughed. "Well, that's one way to describe it, I guess. It's certainly not very elegant looking. It's a gyrocopter, and I designed it. Remember I said I was doing some consulting? Well, that's it."

"Well, I'll be darned," Bud replied, shaking his head. "I've seen that thing around and wondered what the heck it was. And you designed it?"

"I did," Tex replied. "We were on a test flight that day we hovered over you out on the canyon rim. I told George it was poor etiquette, so he moved on. He has a pilot's license and should know better, but he's kind of a loose cannon. But I didn't actually design it from scratch—I guess you could say it's more of a modification of a kit he bought. But it did take some doing."

"Why not just build a standard kit?" Bud asked.

"He wanted one that could carry more people."

"How many can it carry?"

"It's rated for a half-dozen or so, depending on what they weigh. About 1500 pounds. That has to include everything, though, any gear or whatnot."

Bud paused, then said softly, "Well, I'll be a son of a gun. A gyrocopter. And he's the guy who was coming to the cafe every day for a lot of food? Does he have a ton of people working for him?"

"No, it was just me and Allen—I think Allen's still there. He's his property caretaker. I have no idea why he got so much food every day. Maybe he was feeding people in Hanksville, he's like that."

Bud continued, "Do you think he had anything to do with the oboist you found? I mean, he's able to go anywhere, and we found no tracks. Keep in mind I'm just speculating, but you were the only one there at the time."

Tex looked grim, saying, "Sheriff, I really don't know. George is kind of eccentric, but he's no killer. He seems like a nice enough guy, but I just don't know."

"I'm speculating, Tex. That's all it is, just trying to cover all the bases. But when you were telling me and Cal about that night when you heard what we assume was the guy playing the oboe, you mentioned that you heard someone yelling. Could you make out what they were saying?"

"No."

Bud thought of Hattie and the dirt-bike tracks.

"Was it a male voice?"

"Yes."

"And you mentioned hearing a beautiful song. Was it being played on the oboe?"

"I think so."

"Did you recognize the tune?"

"It took me awhile to identify it, but I'm positive it was Ravel's *Boléro.*"

Just then Bud could hear the radio in his vehicle squawking.

"I need to get that," he said. "Hang on."

He was soon back.

"That was the Wayne County Sheriff. I put out an APB on a stolen RV—it belonged to our mayor, Howie. You may remember it from when we came here on our way to the Maze. It appears they've found it. It's out on the property of one George Picco, and they want the owner to come get it and decide if they want to file charges."

Tex replied, "George has no need for an old RV. It must be a mistake."

"Well, I hope you're right," Bud replied. "I need to get back to Green River and tell Howie. You're going to stay here and meet Hattie, then go to Price? Tell her hello for me—and congratulations."

Bud then handed Tex a business card, adding, "And Tex, tell her I'd like to talk to her. She can stop by my office on your way through tomorrow or call me, though I would prefer to talk to her in person—in private."

"Will do," Tex replied, slowly sitting down on a rock, looking thoughtful.

33

Bud had a number of messages on his machine when he got back to the office, the first being a call from Cal telling him he'd only found one thing on Andrew J. Frost, which was a file on him being reported as a missing person, which had later been cancelled by his parents. Cal had also managed to get their phone number.

So, Andy's been on other adventures, Bud mused, chewing on a cinnamon toothpick. He listened to the rest of his messages, which included a call from Wilma Jean telling him to save room for dinner, as they were having company.

Bud groaned. He never enjoyed the thought of having company for dinner, though he knew it would mean having something special to eat. He almost always eventually enjoyed it, once he got over not being able to sit on the back porch and play ball with the dogs, but tonight he wanted to just crawl under the covers. Maybe he should've stayed there when he had the chance earlier, he thought, instead of going to Temple Mountain.

There was a call from Sherwyn telling him he'd gotten in some more Life Savers if he was still interested, as well as a call from Jay, wanting him to come have lunch with him and Chicago Kate tomorrow at the B&B.

But the call that made Bud take note was from Molly out at the Melon View B&B, telling him she was calling on behalf of Andy, who was wondering if Bud could come out and give him a ride into town.

Bud was sure he'd asked Wilma Jean to tell Andy he would pick him up tomorrow for breakfast. He was tired and wanted to go home, and he needed to talk to Howie about the RV. He had no desire to go pick Andy up.

But to his surprise, Andy opened the door just then and came in, sitting in the same chair as the Major had in Bud's dream.

Bud asked, "Is this another dream?"

Andy looked puzzled. "How would I know?"

"Did someone give you a ride?" Bud asked, noting that Andy looked like a different person, his hair combed back and wearing a nice shirt, pants, and a jacket that all looked to be from an LL Bean catalog, though a tad too big.

"I look pretty slick, don't cha think?" Andy asked. "Your wife bought me all this from somewhere. She sure is nice."

Bud now realized Andy was wearing some of his own clothes, things he hadn't worn for years and had forgotten he owned.

"Straight from the Shumway Mercantile," he said, grinning.

"I'm not sure where she got them, but they're sure nice. My clothes needed washing. I asked Molly if I could use her washer, but she said she didn't think the clothes would make it through the first cycle. I had to admit she had a point. She gave me a ride into town."

"How do you like the B&B?" Bud asked.

"It's great," Andy replied. "A bit fancy."

"Well, enjoy it."

"I don't know where I'm going next," Andy said. "I guess I'll be in court soon for murder. I feel real bad about shooting that dog, Bud, as well as his owner. He pulled a gun on me, though."

"Well, that was a long time ago," Bud replied.

"Just how long ago was it?" Andy asked.

"Well, if they laid you to rest in 1882, it was almost 150 years ago."

"No wonder I don't remember it very well. But I can't picture myself shooting a dog. I love dogs."

"Maybe it wasn't really you, Andy, but someone with the same name."

"Oh, it was me, Sheriff. The *Arizona Weekly Enterprise* praised me highly when they wrote my obituary later. They said I was one of Wells Fargo's most trusted messengers who, and I quote, 'In his youth had achieved a very favorable record as one of Powell's men. A frontiersman in the best sense of the word, possessing all the virtues of that class. He was an honest, straightforward everyday man and brave to a fault.'"

"You memorized all that?" Bud asked.

"Wouldn't you if it had been written about you?"

"I guess," Bud answered. "But Andy, we'll figure out a place for you when the time comes. You're not going to jail. I had Cal drop the charges."

"Why in the world would you go do that? I need those charges in order to be found innocent. I can't have that hanging over me."

"There won't be anything hanging over you without any charges. But Andy, I need to ask you a question. Remember when you were up at the Dollhouse, sleeping back between the hoodoos?"

"Sure, I have a good memory. It seems like it was just yesterday."

"It almost was," Bud replied. "But did you hear anything strange up there?"

"Just you guys messing around. I thought you were spooks or something."

"Did you find anything unusual while you were there?"

"No, not that I recall. Oh, wait, I found an oboe case. That's kind of an unusual thing to find out in the desert."

"What did you do with it?"

"I hid it up in the rocks. I had to find a log to get up high enough to make sure it was safe."

"Why were you worried about it being safe?"

"There was a fellow out there wandering around carrying an oboe, and I figured it was his. I was going to tell him where it was, but I never saw him again. He was off in the distance."

Bud wondered if Andy was being forthright with him or was trying to cover up his own involvement in Reece's death.

"Did you open the case?"

"Yes. All it had in it was a folded piece of paper. I didn't look at it."

"Did you notice what this guy was wearing?" Bud asked.

Andy seemed distracted. "No, just some dark clothing."

"And you never got close enough to talk to him?"

"No. Why all the questions? Did something happen to him?"

Bud studied Andy carefully. The oboe case was still in his safe, and he knew he could send it to a lab to see if Andy's prints were on it. But since Andy knew about the case, fingerprints would only prove that Andy had found it, like he had said, nothing else. A lack of his fingerprints would simply mean he was lying, and how could he know about it to lie unless he'd seen it? And he did know what was in it.

Bud was puzzled. How did Andy know it was an oboe case? It seemed to Bud that the average person wouldn't think of an oboe when they saw a case that size, but would think of a flute or clarinet, which were much more common. But then again, he'd said the guy was carrying an oboe. But he'd then said he wasn't close enough to talk to the guy or to even make out clearly what he was wearing. Yet he could clearly make out an oboe, which wasn't all that big of an instrument.

Bud now thought of the mysterious fingerprints on the oboe. Could they be Andy's?

"Do you want to have dinner at my house tonight?" Bud asked.

"Sure. Will your wife be there? She's sure nice. And those others I rode in the car with, they're really good people. They're getting me interested in music again."

"Again?"

Andy hesitated, then said, "I played the snare drum in high-school band."

"I'm not sure who's going to be there. But I need to make a call first," Bud said, dialing Howie's number. "Then we'll head out."

34

Howie had been excited to hear his RV had been found, but was also disappointed that he couldn't go retrieve it immediately. The Wayne County Sheriff had told Bud he'd booted the RV, so Bud assured Howie it would be there the next day.

The RV was soon forgotten in the events of the evening at Bud and Wilma Jean's bungalow, which included a potluck dinner and what Wilma Jean had announced as "musical entertainment" beforehand.

Bud wondered if maybe it had something to do with Jay and Chicago Kate. He didn't know if Kate could play an instrument or sing, but he knew Jay could belt out opera, having heard him.

It was almost dark when Bud pulled up in the drive, discovering he was going to have to park down by the barn, as everywhere else was taken. He felt a little put out—why hadn't his wife told him it was going to be a big party? She'd simply said they were having guests for dinner.

He tried not to let on to Andy he was disgruntled, for he didn't want to spoil anyone else's evening. As he opened the door, he could see the house was bursting with people—their friends Cassie and Shorty, Kale and Molly, Jay and Chicago Kate, Frosty and Mrs. Jensen,

Eldon, and a number of others, all dressed to the nines. Andy immediately went over to hang out with Molly, and Bud knew they would give him a ride back out to the B&B.

He was surprised to see Eldon there, for he knew he hated dinner parties almost as much as Bud did, if not more. It was the first time Bud had seen him dressed up, unless his BOB-O's outfit counted.

Instead of a leisure suit, he wore a dapper-looking suit that reminded Bud a lot of the gangster suit Phil had worn. Wilma Jean must've bribed him with promises of something he liked to eat, Bud figured, slipping into the kitchen to see what was cooking.

He could see the dogs looking in through the screen door, noses working, and Bud was soon outside with them, having snuck a few pieces of salami from a party tray. As far as he was concerned, he could spend the evening out there—well, until dinner was served, anyway.

It wasn't long until Howie found him, eager to learn more about his RV.

"The sheriff says it's down by Hanksville? Can you go with me tomorrow to get it?" He asked.

"I don't think so, Howie," Bud replied. "I need to find Andy a ride back down to Radium, and I also need to talk to Kate Chambers. She and Jay invited me to lunch tomorrow, and I'm also expecting Hattie and Tex to drop by in the morning. I think you could just call the sheriff and have him escort you out there. Maybe get Eldon and Frosty to go along."

"Do you think it's going to be dangerous? Will there be gunplay?"

"Not unless you take a gun along and play with it," Bud laughed. "Just kidding, Mayor," he added. "Usually when a stolen car is retrieved, it's par for the course for the police to have it towed to an impound lot unless the owner comes to get it."

"Impound lot? Where's the nearest one?"

"I don't know, maybe Hanksville. But having it towed won't be cheap, and the sheriff's going to have to be there anyway to remove the boot he put on, so just go out with him. I don't know George Picco personally, but Tex worked for him. I doubt if he's some nefarious criminal."

"He could be a white-collar one. They're the worst sometimes. I wonder if he found the can of beans I left under the hood to warm up."

"White-collar criminals aren't usually given to gunplay. Get Eldon to go. Here he comes, ask him."

"Ask him what?" Eldon asked, closing the screen door behind him. "You guys hiding out here? Can I join you? I hate dinner parties —except for the dinner part."

"Remember what I said, Eldon," Howie replied. "Lemonade, my friend, lemonade."

"What's that supposed to mean?" Bud asked.

"Eldon's so mad at Frosty it's starting to turn into rage."

"I'm mad," Eldon admitted, "But not *that* mad."

Howie continued, ignoring him. "I told him to make lemonade out of lemons. He needs a way to let out the anger instead of holding it in where it will slowly eat him away like a worm in a watermelon."

"I don't hold it in, dang it, Howie. I have plenty of outbursts. You can ask anybody in Green River."

"Have you been practicing?" Howie asked. "This is the night of reckoning."

With that, he went back inside, leaving Eldon and Bud on the porch.

"What in hellsbells is that all about?" Bud asked, half-afraid to hear the answer.

Eldon eased down into a wicker chair across from him, unbuttoning his suit jacket.

"I made the mistake of writing this little poem—or whatever you want to call it—the other day when I was letting off steam. Howie just happened along at the wrong time, and I made my second mistake by showing it to him. I've never written a poem before. I've been practicing writing as a form of what he's calling rage therapy. I'm not that mad, Bud, just a little put out, and I'm actually getting over it."

"So what exactly is the problem?"

"He made it into a song and bribed me into playing it tonight. He says I started a new music genre. He's calling it Rage Band music, like Garage Band but without the "Ga" part, and he says it's going to make me famous. I don't want to be famous."

"Man, he must've had a good bribe to get you to perform in public."

"He promised me his RV."

"Did he tell you it's been stolen?"

"I just now learned that," Eldon replied. "I heard him mention it to someone inside. It's a dirty trick, and I'm not gonna do it."

"Did you know there's a rep from the Chicago Symphony here, as well as Jay?"

"I'm going to be the laughingstock of Green River if I sing that song."

"You *did* get all dressed up. I think it would be good for you to sing it, get rid of some of that rage. You know Frosty's here tonight, you can look directly at him as you're singing."

Bud was trying hard not to laugh. They'd never had a concert in their living room before, Bud mused, or anywhere on the property, for that matter. He wondered how Wilma Jean would take it—or was this the entertainment she'd mentioned?

"Anyway, if you do it I'll buy you lunch every day for a week at the Melon Rind."

"Seriously?" Eldon asked, standing and re-buttoning his jacket.

"Yes, and you know my word is good, unlike some politicians we both know."

They both went back inside, the dogs following along, Bud hoping his wife wouldn't notice them. The talk was now getting louder, the wine starting to kick in.

Seeing them, Howie announced, "Folks, we have a little concert here for you tonight. Our esteemed BOB-O leader is going to sing for us. Tell us the name of your song, Eldon."

Eldon walked to the front of the living room and said, nervously, "I Don't Care."

Howie asked, "You don't care if we know the name?"

"No, I Don't Care. C'mon, Howie, you know what it is."

"I Don't Care?" Howie asked.

"Right. Me neither," Eldon said, getting flustered.

Howie smiled, saying, "This is a song Eldon wrote in the new Rage Band tradition, which is a derivative of punk rock. I wrote the tune and will play my guitar while Shorty plays stick."

Bud's geologist friend Shorty, who was anything but short, held up a stick, grinning.

"Hit it boys," Howie demanded, and Shorty began tapping a rhythm on a glass with the stick while Eldon looked half-sick, Bud nodding at him encouragingly.

Howie soon cut in with a guitar lick that sounded to Bud like the tune from *A Tisket, A Tasket*, but with a whining sound behind it.

Now Eldon started chanting in his raspy voice, and though it was hard to hear him at first, he glanced at Frosty and soon ramped up the volume in a kind of sing-song.

> I don't care what you drive,
> I don't care what you wear,
> I don't care for your new wife,
> I just don't care.

Bud glanced over at Jay and Kate. Jay looked resigned, like he'd been here before, but Kate looked slightly horrified. Howie was now trying to make the guitar squeal as Eldon got louder and louder. Bud saw the dogs head for the bedroom.

> I don't care what you say,
> I don't care about your day,
> It wouldn't matter anyway,
> I just don't care.

Wilma Jean and Maureen left the room, going back into the kitchen, as Shorty whacked the glass so hard that Bud was sure it would break. Cassie, previously sitting next to Shorty, ducked back behind him and was holding her sides, trying not to let Eldon see she was laughing.

> I don't care,
> I don't care,
> Did I mention I don't care?

Instead of the glass breaking, it was the stick, pieces flying through the room, everyone ducking. Eldon finished the last lines while Howie played the same three high notes over and over.

> I don't care,
> I don't care,
> I just donnnn't caaaare.

Howie threw his guitar onto the carpet and shouted, "Don't care!" then stomped a few times, trying to act bad.

Maureen came out from the kitchen, giving Howie a look, then said, "We don't throw guitars around in this house, Mr. Mayor," then handed him his guitar. Everyone laughed, thinking she was part of the act.

Now everyone started clapping, Frosty and Eileen Jensen laughing. But Eldon was long gone, hiding out on the porch, though Bud knew he wouldn't leave until he'd eaten dinner.

35

Bud went to bed late, the party taking some time to wind down. One of the last to leave was Eldon, and he and Frosty walked out the door with their arms around each other's shoulders while Mrs. Jensen looked on approvingly, walking with what Bud thought looked like a bit of a tilt from the wine.

Finally settled in, he'd gone right to sleep until his wife had gently elbowed him, waking him from snoring, which he did only when he was especially tired.

Deciding to give her a break, he grabbed a blanket and pillow and went and slept on the couch, Lindie at his feet, the boys staying in the comfy bed.

He soon woke again, this time to a sound he'd heard only a few times before out in the deep canyons, a sound that chilled him to his very bones. His first thought upon hearing the scream was to wonder if he'd locked the doors, and his second was to wonder about the safety of the two horses in the pasture next door.

He'd no more than decided to go check on them in his FJ when he looked up to see a face in the window above the couch—the face of a very large mountain lion. He instinctively rolled off the couch onto the floor, then got up and ran to the bedroom where he kept his gun in a safe in the closet, unlocking it and taking out his Remington 700 rifle, which he rarely used.

He was sure his wife and the dogs would be awakened by the lion scream or by his rummaging about in the dark, but nobody seemed bothered. Even Lindie still slept, never having made a move, even with him rolling off the couch.

It had to have been a dream, Bud thought, closing the curtain and crawling back under the blanket. But try as he might, he couldn't go back to sleep, tossing and turning.

What if it *had* been real? He wondered again about the horses in the nearby field, though he knew that lions rarely attacked horses, as deer and smaller animals were more their style, horses being harder to take down. And it was equally rare to see a lion in Green River, though he knew they followed the deer down to the lower country in the fall.

And mountain lions never looked in people's windows, Bud thought. Yet he recalled reading a story about a young lad back in the 1800s who was alone on a ranch in Colorado and had one try to get in the cabin window. It might be extremely rare, but he knew a curious lion unafraid of humans might look in.

Feeling chilled, partly from fear and partly from the night, he got up again and went around turning on lights both inside and outside the house. He put on his boots and coat, grabbed his rifle, a flashlight, and the FJ keys, then slipped out the front door, immediately blinded by the porch light.

He would get inside the FJ where it was safe and drive around, seeing if he could spot the lion, even though he suspected it was long gone.

Remembering he'd had to park down by the barn, he almost went back inside, but instead slowly made his way down to the shadows where the FJ sat, watching behind him, as he knew lions took their prey from behind, typically breaking their necks.

Bud never locked the FJ when home, and he was glad he didn't have to fumble with the keys in the dark, instead opening the door and jumping inside. Slamming the FJ door, he sat for a moment, breathing hard, until he panicked, wondering if the lion had somehow gotten inside the vehicle.

He scanned the interior with his flashlight, then realizing how terrified he was, sat and took deep breaths until his heart rate slowed a bit. Cold, he turned on the FJ and let it warm up, then turned the heater on full blast.

The heat felt good, warming him back up, and he turned on the radio, trying to regain a feeling of normalcy. Patsy Kline was belting out *I Fall to Pieces*, which was followed by, of all things, C.W. McCall's *Convoy*.

> We got a little ol' convoy,
> Rockin' through the night,
> Yeah, we got a little ol' convoy,
> Ain't she a beautiful sight?

Bud relaxed, smiling. He hadn't heard the song for years, and it seemed odd that it would come on now, of all times, in the middle of the night while he sat listening to the radio.

And why exactly was he out here? Oh, yes, looking for a mountain lion, he remembered, turning the FJ's lights on.

He backed out, scanning the fields for movement as he drove, turning onto the main road, though it was hard to see anything, as a fog had settled in from the passing storm. He was soon near the field with the horses, where his headlights showed them peacefully grazing.

The lion obviously hadn't come that direction, so he turned around, heading back the other way, passing the lit-up bungalow. He didn't see any movement inside, so he figured Wilma Jean and the dogs were still sleeping.

The song over, Bud found another station, this one playing an old Marty Robbins' song.

> A white sports coat and a pink carnation,
> I'm all dressed up for the dance.

He quickly changed stations. He knew that song well, and he also knew it would become an earworm, bothering him all day. He dialed in a talk station:

Affirmations play an integral role in the healing journey. We have to truly and completely love and accept ourselves, then everything we need will be on its way.

And you really believe that?

Of course I do. Are you challenging my heartfelt beliefs?

Can you prove that they work?

Of course I can. Didn't you see the fancy limo that I came here in?

Bud grinned, again changing the station, this time to what appeared to be classical.

And that was Beethoven's Tenth Symphony. We hope you enjoyed it. Stay tuned for a word from our sponsor, then we'll be listening to Schoenberg's Five Orchestral Pieces, his most-important atonal composition. If you're having trouble sleeping, get ready for a good snooze.

Beethoven's Tenth? Hadn't Howie said Beethoven had never finished it?

Bud pulled over, now sure he was dreaming. It was then that he saw movement in the ditch next to him, and a pair of eyes reflected yellow in the FJ's lights, looking directly at him.

He reached for his rifle, but hesitated. He knew it was the lion from the size and height of the eyes, but he had no intention of aiming at something in the dark, especially something he could only make out the eyes of. He didn't want to kill it anyway, just scare it off.

He opened the FJ window, pushed the barrel of the rifle out, aimed it at the sky, then pulled the trigger, ready for the recoil. The noise was deafening, and he immediately regretted shooting the gun, his ears ringing. He was sure now it wasn't a dream.

The eyes had disappeared, and he could soon see lights coming on in nearby houses. He turned around and headed back to the bungalow, wishing he'd never gotten out of bed, for he knew he would soon be getting calls about someone shooting in the dark and would be wishing it *had* all been a dream.

36

Bud sat at his desk, trying not to think of the steady gaze of the lion's eyes watching him through the window the previous night, hoping it had moved on. For some reason, the whole event had shaken him up way more than it normally would have.

He wondered if it could've possibly been the one Andy said he'd seen down at the Dollhouse. He knew it was highly improbable, yet he knew lions could have territories of several hundred miles, depending on food sources. It would be interesting if it were the same one, he mused, but there was no way he would ever know.

Could the yelling Tex had heard from the cliff been Reece trying to fend off a lion the night he'd been killed? Had Reece pulled out his oboe and started playing weird noises to distract the animal from killing him? Bud had read about a man who was being mauled by a grizzly and had his phone ring, the ringtone being a song by Metallica, which had made the grizzly run. An oboe might have the same effect on a lion, he mused.

He made a pot of coffee, still sleepy from the night before. Sipping the hot brew, he wondered where Phil Baker was, feeling a tad guilty for basically running him off the previous day, yet hoping he didn't show back up.

He first returned the several calls on his answering machine from the night before, telling them he'd been the source of the shot and was trying to scare off a lion. He wanted people to be aware and keep their pets indoors for the next few days, yet he didn't want to alarm anyone. After all, it hadn't been in town, but out in the country where the deer hung out, which was perfectly normal for a lion.

Bud next made a few other calls, then was dialing Howie to see if he was on his way to Hanksville when the door opened.

Putting the phone back down, Bud could see it was Hattie.

"Good morning, Hattie. Have a seat. Want a cup of coffee?"

"Sure," she replied. Bud could see she was nervous, but he figured he would be too if the sheriff had asked him to stop by, giving no reason.

"Congratulations on your new life," Bud said, handing her a cup of coffee. "Cream?"

"No thanks," she replied. "Tex is waiting outside in the truck, Bud. He said you wanted to talk to me alone."

"I do, Hattie, and I'll get right to it. I don't know if he told you about the fellow we found dead in the Dollhouse, but I wanted to ask you a few questions about it."

Bud watched as she shifted in her seat, looking even more nervous.

"He told me about it, Sheriff, and I'll be glad to tell you what I know."

Bud was surprised. He'd half-thought she wouldn't have anything to say about it. After all, lots of people rode dirt bikes in the canyon country, even though November was starting to get too cold. He hadn't known if it was even her.

She now started talking a mile a minute.

"I was in there, just messing around. I'd never seen the Dollhouse, and I thought it would make a great day outing. Since it was a mid-week, I figured there wouldn't be many people coming by the cafe, so I packed a lunch and off I went. I did tell Robin, my ranger friend, where I was going in case something happened. I had also packed overnight gear just in case."

Bud asked, "You just take off into the backcountry like that on your own and think nothing of it?"

"Sure. I grew up riding dirt bikes and exploring on my own. I usually tell someone and also carry supplies if I'm going to be out long. And I know how to fix most of the stuff on my bike. So yeah, I like to go exploring. I'm also armed, by the way."

Bud nodded, and Hattie continued.

"Anyway, I was having a great time until I came across this fellow wearing a tuxedo. He was carrying a small case with him, and nothing else, not even water. It was just so weird. He asked if I could help him, and I gave him some of my water. He was actually in pretty bad shape, to the point I didn't think he could ride out with me on the bike since the road was so rough, he was so weak. He couldn't even keep the water down."

Bud was surprised at what she was telling him. It looked like maybe Hattie was the last one to see Reece alive, other than his possible killer, and Bud was anxious to hear what she could tell him.

"It was so odd. I mean, to meet a guy in a tux with no supplies way out there? He was lucky it wasn't hot, or he would've been history in that outfit—well, I guess he was history anyway."

"Go ahead," Bud said.

"I told him to go up on this high spot where he would be pretty visible, and I would ride back out and get him help. The guy was too weak to even hardly walk, so I gave him a ride up to the top of this small cliff where he would be visible. He barely stayed on my bike. The plan was to go to the Hans Flat Ranger Station and get help, get a chopper in there."

"That explains why we saw dirt-bike tracks but no people tracks," Bud replied. "The scuff marks on top probably covered what tracks he did leave. And he definitely was carrying the case when you took him to the top?"

"Yes, and then he explained that he was part of a group that had come into the canyons to look for a place to hold a concert, which I found really weird. When I asked where the others were, he said they were being mean to him because he was the oboe player. That made even less sense. But he said he'd left, then couldn't find his way back to rejoin them. Apparently they'd come in at Spanish Bottom on a raft, and he couldn't find the trail back down there."

She continued. "So, I hightailed it out and rode as quickly as possible to Hans Flat, but there was no one there, so I kept going to Goblin Valley. As you know, it's a long ride, and it was hours before I got there. Robin got ahold of the Canyonlands rangers, but they said they couldn't do a search and rescue after dark, especially one on the other side of the Golden Stairs. There was nothing we could do but wait until morning. I questioned whether or not the guy would even make it through the night, and I still wish I'd tried to bring him out on my bike, though I guess I should respect my judgement at the time. I didn't think he could stay on my little Honda 250."

Hattie sipped the coffee, then continued. "Well, I figured I'd done what I could, but I checked with Robin the next day and she said they'd never even called her back for a location. Someone dropped the ball."

Bud said, "They had a dignitary visiting and were swamped. That's why I got involved, though by then it was a body recovery. They called the Radium Sheriff, who called me. Someone said later the Vice President had been visiting."

Hattie replied, "I wanted to go back in, but there was nothing I could do, and I figured someone was on it anyway. I thought about that poor guy all day, then the next day, you and Tex showed up and I found out he'd died. I felt terrible."

"Hattie, you were apparently one of the last ones to see him alive."

"I had nothing to do with his death, Sheriff, you have to understand that. I was trying to help him."

She leaned forward in her chair, hands over her face, and started crying.

"It's OK, Hattie," Bud said. "You did your best. That's all any of us can ever do. But did you see anyone else back in there?"

"No, but I found out later that Tex was there not long after me, but he didn't know the guy was up there. He told me all about hearing the weird sounds, though."

"Did he say what he thought they might be?"

"Maybe the guy playing his oboe."

"In the dark on top of a rock when he was almost dead from exposure?"

"I don't know. People do weird things when they're dying."

"Would you have any reason to think Tex might have been involved somehow?"

Hattie looked horrified. "Tex? No way."

Bud stood and went to where Hattie sat, putting his hand on her shoulder. "It's OK, Hattie. I think I know what happened, and it didn't have anything to do with you or Tex. I appreciate you coming in here. I have to cover all the bases. I hope you understand."

Hattie stood, saying, "Bud, thanks for sharing that with me. I've felt so awful lately. Do you know anything about this guy?"

"Yes, his name was Reece Billings, and he was an oboist with the Chicago Symphony. His sister's here in town."

"What happened to him?" She asked. "Did he die of exposure?"

"No, I don't think so, though I'm sure that contributed to his inability to think clearly and thereby protect himself."

He was ready to tell her that Reece fell, but had second thoughts, as he knew she would blame herself for taking him up on the cliff.

"Hattie, you go on up to Price and get that restaurant going. I'll come up one of these days and tell you how this turns out."

She turned, dried her eyes, and left, Bud now pretty sure he knew what had caused Reece Billings to tumble off the cliff, and he knew it wasn't human.

37

It was almost noon, and Bud slipped into the nice tweed jacket he'd brought for the luncheon at the Wandering One B&B with Chicago Kate and Jay, the jacket about as close to dressing up as he ever got.

He was looking forward to the lunch in some ways, hoping Jay would serve his delicious lasagna, yet he was dreading it, for he knew it was time to tell Kate about her brother.

Just then, Howie and Eldon walked in, and Bud knew immediately something was different from the tone in Howie's voice.

"Sheriff, we went down to Hanksville and got my RV, though we didn't actually get it," Howie said excitedly. "Man, you should see this guy's setup. Is he an airplane nut or what? Hangers, runways, even wind flags."

"They're called wind socks," Eldon interjected.

Ignoring him, Howie continued, "And sure enough, there was my RV, parked right next to a trailer that sure looked like the one at the Temple Mountain Cafe."

"The one that *used* to be at the Temple Mountain Cafe," Bud corrected him.

"It's the same one?" Howie asked. "Does Hattie know her trailer's been stolen? Man, this guy's worse than I thought."

"He bought it from her," Bud said. "But was the sheriff out there with you?"

"No, he gave us the key and told us to go get the boot and bring it back to his office. I got the impression he didn't want to deal with it."

Bud wondered if George Picco hadn't made a few contributions to the Wayne County Sheriff's Department.

"Did he do anything about the fact the guy stole it?" Bud asked.

"He didn't actually steal it," Howie replied, to which Eldon interrupted, saying, "Money did all the talking on this one, Sheriff."

Howie continued, looking irritated. "The guy who had it said he thought it had been abandoned out there for a long time."

"To his credit, it did look the part," Eldon added.

"He saw it while flying around in his gyrocopter. He flew his helper guy in to get it," Howie said.

"That would explain the pod tracks we saw. And they hot wired it?" Bud asked.

Howie looked even more irritated. "I didn't ask. He did what anyone would do, Sheriff."

"That's why it's illegal, right?" Eldon asked. "You can just say a vehicle looks abandoned, then take it home with you. Everyone does it."

Bud was confused. "What exactly happened? Did you get the RV or not?"

"Howie sold it to the guy, Bud," Eldon said. "We all thought this Picco guy was the thief, but in the end, it turned out to be our very own mayor. He made out like a bandit."

Bud was incredulous. "I hope he made it worth your time, Howie, especially since he did basically steal it."

Howie grinned, sitting down and putting his feet up on Bud's desk. "Now I can afford a real RV, though I'm not sure I want another one. He gave me ten grand for it, Bud."

Bud whistled. "Ten grand? How much did you pay for it?"

"Eight-hundred buckaroos. But see, he didn't steal it from me because it's not technically mine yet. I just sent the title in to be changed, and it hasn't come back yet."

"So who does it belong to, then?" Eldon asked.

"Government limbo land," Howie replied. "But he paid me and I wrote out a bill of sale, and when the new title comes, I'll sign it and mail it to him. He didn't seem too worried. He knows I'm mayor here."

"Finding out you're a politician should make him even more worried," Eldon added.

"Why would a guy with lots of money want an old RV?" Bud asked.

"He said he wants it to pull his Bowlus trailer 'cause they match. He likes old antique stuff," Howie said.

"But Sheriff, I have even bigger news," Howie added. "We found the missing orchestra—well, the missing quintet, I should say."

"It would be a quartet now, Howie, with the oboe player gone."

"No, it's still a quintet. The raft guide's with them. He plays guitar. They played their version of Beethoven's Fifth for us. Have you ever heard the intro notes played on a bass guitar? Dum da da duuum. It was kind of cool."

"They played Beethoven's Fifth as a quintet?" Bud asked. "And the guitarist is the guy from the Green River Waterways?"

"Yes. They've all been staying out at Picco's place, living high on the hog. He's been flying them around in his gyrocopter, looking for the best place for a concert. He picked them up down on the river some time ago."

Bud replied, "That explains people hearing music in the canyons, and that's who Hattie's been feeding all this time. But did they mention why the oboe player hadn't been with them? Do they even know he's dead?"

"They said he told them he was going to walk out, and they weren't worried. They said he was in good shape. They're city folks, Bud, and I don't think they have the vaguest clue what that would entail. But Picco's also from Chicago, and I guess he knows them, as they're all on a first name basis. He's a classical music buff. I asked them if they knew we'd been looking for them, and they acted surprised, saying they'd all been in contact with their families."

"That's why Reece's sister Kate got worried. He hadn't been in contact. But is Picco the guy who gave them the grant to bring music to us poor impoverished souls out here?"

"I don't know," Howie said. "But it wouldn't surprise me."

"We're not impoverished," Eldon replied. "We've got Howie and the Ramblin' Road Rangers, not to mention my new band. By the way, I'd like to collect on that first meal at the Melon Rind today."

"OK, but I can't join you," Bud replied. "I already have a lunch date. Just tell Maureen or Wilma Jean it's on me."

"I think I'll treat our mayor, too," Eldon said. "Though he should be treating us, since he's rich now—a deal's a deal, Bud."

"Just put it on my tab," Bud replied. He could now see Andy coming down the street. "And take Andy, too. But I need to go, fellas."

They all left, and as Bud locked up the office, he thought back on the pen Hattie had given him with Picco's name on it, as well as the card in Reece's pocket. It all made sense, now, but why was there a check in the oboe case for almost a quarter-million dollars with Picco's signature?

Even though he felt he now had a good idea what had happened to Reece, he knew there were some loose ends he needed to tie up, and these could definitely make a difference in how everything turned out.

Bud jumped in the FJ and headed for Jay's, the oboe case beside him. He dreaded what would come next—the task of telling Chicago Kate her brother was dead.

38

Jay had indeed made lasagna, knowing it was Bud's favorite, and after lunch and some small talk, he'd excused himself to go run errands in town, knowing Bud wanted to talk to Kate about her brother.

"He's sure a gem of a guy," Kate said, watching Jay get in his car and drive off.

"That he is," agreed Bud. "And a good cook, too."

"I'm hoping to come back and visit again soon," Kate said. "I've also invited him to come to Chicago. I hope he does."

She looked kind of distant, as if contemplating dinner at some fancy Chicago restaurant with a famous opera singer.

Bud said, "Kate, tell me about your brother. You said everyone hated him. Could you elaborate on that?"

She leaned back, then said, "Well, it all has to do with being an oboe player. See, the oboe is the center of the orchestra."

"I would've thought that would be the conductor," Bud said.

Kate replied, "So would the conductor, but if everyone's out of tune you can't play. And without tuning to the oboe, you can't properly tune an orchestra, well, unless there's no oboe, but then it wouldn't be a proper orchestra."

"Why can't you tune to some other instrument?" Bud asked.

"Well, you know at the start of any concert, the oboe first plays an A note, which is the standard tuning note, followed by the other instruments playing an A. Most instruments can be tuned anytime anyplace, but the oboe can't. The only way to alter the pitch of an oboe is to adjust the reeds, which is very difficult and not something you want to do at the start of a concert. So, the other instruments are tuned to the oboe."

She continued. "This in itself is enough to make the other orchestra members hate them, but oboists are very aware of all this and thus tend to be quite narcissistic. And they can be very detail-oriented and obsessive, but most people don't realize they have to make their own reeds. And oboe is so hard to play—on a good day it's a swan, poignant, rich, and complex, but on a bad day it's a really sick duck. And so, everyone always hates the oboist—it's a classical tradition."

She paused, then continued. "But my brother Reece was the kindest, most gentle oboe player you'll ever meet. And so, even though everyone loved him outside of when they were playing, he was hated in the orchestral arena because he broke the mold—he was not only an oboist, but a *nice* oboist. Plus, he was quite talented. They were jealous."

"Jealous enough to kill him?" Bud asked.

"Yes, but classical musicians don't kill people outright, they have other methods. Have you ever heard Wellington's Victory by —yes—Beethoven? It's bombastic and quotes tunes like 'God Save the King' and calls for artillery sound effects. It's been called cheesy."

"I always find artillery sound effects to be cheesy," Bud replied. "Excepting at military funerals, of course. But what about those burros in the Grand Canyon Suite?"

She looked surprised. "I didn't know you were into classical."

Bud dodged, saying, "And of course that composer who used an oboe to portray a duck."

"Peter and the Wolf!" Kate said. "And Beethoven used three different kinds of birds in his famous Symphony No. 6, the *Pastoral*.

The flute was the nightingale, the oboe was the quail, and two alternating clarinets made the sounds of the cuckoo."

Bud replied, "And did you know the third largest crater on Mercury is named in honor of Beethoven, as is an asteroid?"

"I'm quite impressed. And here I thought no one out here in the hinterlands appreciated classical. Now I find Jay and you both do."

Bud kept going. "And did you know that Stravinsky's *Rite of Spring* caused a riot at its premiere in France? It was too radical for them. It should've been called *Riot of Spring*."

"Stravinsky conducted the Chicago Symphony," Kate said proudly. "He conducted in 1940 for the premiere of his *Symphony in C,* but of course that was before my time."

Bud added, "Stravinsky later became an American citizen."

Kate sighed. "You certainly know a lot about classical music. I've gotten to meet lots of well-known musicians and conductors. And of course Solti and Muti. They're both famous conductors with the Chicago Symphony, in case you don't know. I'm on a first-name basis with Muti, but not Solti, as he's dead."

Feeling this was as good of a segue as he was going to get, Bud said, "Kate, I need to tell you something about your brother."

"Oh, I know he's passed," she replied. "The police came to my house the night before I came out here."

"So you've known all along? I was hesitant to tell you when you first arrived, as my wife said you were enjoying yourself."

"I've been trying to distract myself. I've been going in and out of denial, though I've been doing a lot of grieving, too. Jay knows, he's a real gentleman and has been helping a lot."

"He has some good red wine, at least according to my wife, since I don't drink much," Bud said.

"I know that. I *do* know that."

Bud now took the oboe case from the bag it was in and handed it to Kate, saying, "This is Reece's case. It was found near his body, as was his oboe. The medical lab has the oboe and has your address, so will send it along. We needed to make sure there weren't any unknown fingerprints on it."

"Were there?" She asked.

"They did find fingerprints that weren't Reece's, but we can't ID them."

"I hope they're careful with his oboe. It's a professional Yamaha and was quite expensive."

She opened the case, taking out the musical score and examining it, saying, "I'm not at all surprised to find this. Reece fancied himself somewhat of a composer. He was infatuated with Beethoven and had decided to try to finish his Tenth Symphony. I knew Reece well enough to know he had no grand delusions—it was just an exercise in creativity for him. And did you know a fellow did just finish it, using computers?"

"That would explain why I heard the tail end of it on the radio. But how would that work?" Bud asked.

She continued. "First, a fellow named Barry Cooper took all the fragments Beethoven had left and put them together, trying to stay true to Beethoven's style. His score was first performed at a concert given in 1988 by the Royal Philharmonic Society in London, who Beethoven had offered the new symphony to in 1827 while still composing it. But just recently, artificial intelligence was used to reconstruct the third and fourth movement of the symphony. It was just premiered."

"Interesting. But what do you think about the note about the airport and locker?" Bud asked.

"Well, as for the Salt Lake City Airport notation, I'm sure it was Reece's way of reminding himself he was flying out of there. He flew around so much. He once told me he'd wake up in the night sweating, wondering where he was and if he was going to miss his next flight. Poor guy. I always felt he should've been a writer. He would've been much happier writing by a fireplace in his PJs."

"As for the note about the locker, he told me he'd stored some of his personal items in the lockers at the raft place. He didn't want to take them down the river. That's what the combination is for. He said he left his billfold, phone, and plane ticket. I need to go get them."

"Do you have any idea why was he wearing a tuxedo out in the canyons?" Bud asked.

"My brother was also a fan of the composer Brahms, who always dressed up to compose, even when he was alone. Reece thought that by dressing in a tux to play, he was giving it his finest, as well as showing respect for the composer. So he always wore a tux when he played, no matter where or for who. And he insisted that anyone playing with him dress the same, which of course added to his unpopularity—but he was the oboist, so whatever he said must be obeyed."

Bud now pulled the check from beneath the velveteen liner, handing it to her. "Any idea what this would be for?"

"Oh my gosh! It's the missing check! We knew it was supposed to go to Reece, as he was the symphony secretary, but it had just disappeared. This is the grant money I was telling you about."

"Well, so much for my theories," Bud said.

"What were your theories?" Kate asked.

"I had a very elaborate scam made up where Reece was selling a valuable manuscript to George Picco, leaving it in a locker in the Salt Lake City Airport—or some such thing."

Kate laughed. "That's very creative, but you didn't know Reece. He would never do anything like that. But Sheriff, can you tell me what happened to him? How did he die? I've been hesitant to ask, as I'm not sure I really want to know, especially if it was painful."

"There was only one potential witness, and he didn't actually see anything, but heard someone playing noise on the oboe, followed by music, then yelling. But let me back up. Reece was shunned by the other musicians on this raft trip for making them all wear tuxedos while playing, or maybe for some other reason, I'm not sure until I can actually talk to them."

"They didn't need any reason other than him playing oboe, Bud. But they're not bad people, just traditional."

"The Maze is one of the most tortured landscapes you'll ever see, Kate. Reece apparently got lost and wandered around. A woman who was riding her dirt bike found him, but she wasn't able to take him out with her, so she went for help. She said he was terribly dehydrated. I can give you her number if it would help give you any closure. It was soon dark, Reece was weak, and a lion found him and decided it would be an opportunity it couldn't pass up."

"That's terrible!"

"It would be, but we didn't find any marks on his body. I think he was trying to flee the lion and instead fell off a cliff. If it's any consolation, he died quickly."

Bud added, "But Kate, he had one final moment of beauty. We think he tried to scare it off by making loud sounds with his oboe, but after that, he was able to play one last beautiful piece of classical music—*Boléro*. It was one final peaceful moment for him. He then started yelling and backed off the cliff."

Kate looked alarmed. "Reece hated Ravel's *Boléro*. He called it the ultimate ear worm. He hate-hate-hated *Boléro*. He almost got into fisticuffs with other musicians who would argue that Ravel was a great composer."

"Hated *Boléro*? Do you have any idea why?" Bud asked, surprised.

"I think it had to do with an incident when he was with the Cleveland Orchestra. He misread the music during a concert and ended up playing his part at the wrong time. Nobody in the audience knew the difference, but it was hugely humiliating to him. After that, he would always say that *Boléro* was just the same thing over and over. And in a way, it is. He said a monkey could play it. I think he associated it with this bad experience, but a lot of musicians hate *Boléro*. Ravel wasn't well when he composed it, I'm sure you know. It was one of his last compositions."

"Did they ever figure out what was wrong with him?" Bud asked.

Kate replied, "They think he had progressive primary aphasia, which erodes the brain's language centers. He gradually lost the ability to speak, write, and play the piano. The left side of his brain was failing. Musical abilities are spread throughout the brain—different areas deal with pitch, melody, harmony, and rhythm. Ravel lost the ability to create real music using all its components. He even himself said that *Boléro* wasn't real music. It contains only two themes, each repeated eight times. But it has 30 superimposed lines and 25 different combinations of sounds. Ravel himself described it as 'an orchestral fabric without music.'"

"It's sure repetitive," Bud commented.

"Ravel became interested in machinery at the end of his life, which could account for that," Kate said. "I personally find it mesmerizing and could listen to it over and over. It showcases each instrument so beautifully. But in any case, there was no way my brother would have played *Boléro*. Someone else had to be there or your witness misheard."

"Either's possible," Bud replied. "In any case, it's food for thought. But Kate I need to make a call. These guys will help you make arrangements for the body."

He handed her the number of the Radium mortuary and left.

As much as he liked Kate, he was happy that was over. And now, he needed to find that number Cal had given him for Andy Frost's parents, because he had a few questions for them, his lion theory having just bit the dust.

39

There seemed to be no end to this wood, and no beginning, and no difference in it, and, worst of all, no way out.

Howie was reading from *The Wind in the Willows* to a rapt audience in the Melon Rind Cafe, Bud among them. The cafe's two back booths held Bud, Howie, Eldon, Frosty, Eileen Jensen, Andy, Maureen, and Wilma Jean, though the latter two were up and down, waiting on customers.

After lunch at Jay's, Bud had gone back to his office, called Andy's folks, then gone to the cafe to see if Andy was there.

Wanda had just delivered the mail, which included that day's *New York Times*, and even though it was actually a few days' previous edition, no one cared. Wilma Jean had a subscription and would set the paper out in an effort to keep everyone up on the news, though most considered Wanda's sidewalk news more interesting.

Standing at the counter reading the paper, Wilma Jean interrupted Howie, saying, "Hey, there's an article here about that guy who was always asking everyone questions. Listen to this."

Chicagoan Predicts What the Future Holds

Phil Baker studies the future and claims to know what it holds. Baker's what's called a futurist, and his Chicago company, Future Holdings, claims to be able to tell you what's going to happen, at least in terms of what future trends will be.

When asked what a futurist actually is, Baker said he prefers to be known as a horizon scanner, someone who explores how the future emerges from the present. He spends most of his time in the field, asking people questions to determine how their preferences will influence future trends.

So far, Baker has an 85% accuracy rate, which makes his many clients very happy. "The only reason I don't have a 100% accuracy rate," claims Baker, "Is because sometimes people don't know what they want in the future, making it hard to predict. They change their minds a lot."

Baker's extensive client list consists primarily of manufacturers, marketers and advertisers, movie producers, politicians, and inventors.

When asked to name some of his successful predictions, Baker says, "I predicted the staycation, where people stay home or nearby to vacation, as well as the disposable diaper. I also predicted the use of carbon dioxide in candies to make things fizzle, resulting in things like Pop Rocks. Other predictions include plastic flowers and drive-through espresso stands."

What does Baker see in our future? When asked, he said, "We are in the midst of a historical transformation. People are going back to the good old days more and more, and I foresee clothing trends following, with old fashions becoming popular again. Vintage and second-hand stores will flourish. Down-to-earth rockabilly music will also become hugely popular, as well as old-fashioned peppermint candies. If you own an older vehicle, be prepared for it to increase in value as people yearn for and try to recreate the past. In addition, you'll see older members of society getting out for adventures, as well as marrying or remarrying at older ages. The wedding industry will not benefit from this, however, as these people will have small outdoor weddings or elope. Rural areas will become the cat's meow as people leave the cities, which I myself am in the process of doing."

When asked to name some of his predictions that didn't make it, Baker laughed and said, "Disposable socks, that X and Q would be dropped from the alphabet, that books would disappear, and that everyone would be able to predict the future."

In short, Baker says it's a good day to be indigenous, an even better time to be alive, and the future will always be there for us.

Everyone shook their heads in amazement except Eldon, who said, "I knew he was up to something. Stealing our ideas and selling them—what a rascal!"

"He didn't steal nuthin'," Frosty argued. "He listened and observed and synthesized it all together. It takes a lot more than just asking questions to do what he does, Eldon."

"Are you and Eileen going to elope?" Eldon asked.

"If you're gonna play that 'I don't care' song at the wedding we will," Frosty replied.

Bud knew they were just getting started, and he leaned over to Andy, who sat across from him, and asked, "You want to go to the river museum? It has a neat old dory."

Andy nodded yes, and the pair slipped out of the booth and through the cafe door. They were soon in Bud's FJ and on their way to the museum, which sat on the banks of the Green River.

40

After wandering around the museum for awhile, Bud said, "Let's go look at the ducks, Andy."

They went out on the walk to the middle of the bridge across the Green, then stood, leaning against the guard rail, looking down into the slow-moving dark water below.

The river was low, and they could see filagrees of ice forming along its edges. Ducks swam in the rushes and tall grasses, poking their heads underwater every so often.

Andy said, "It's funny how they swim in a row."

"Like little convoys," Bud replied.

They stood for the longest time, silent, immersed in their own thoughts. A great blue heron glided down into the water, and they watched it in silence.

"It sure is a graceful bird for looking so gawky," Andy remarked.

"That it is," Bud replied. "But Andy, I think it's time to go home. Your mom and dad just paid for a ticket, and my wife said she'd fly you down to the airport in Radium later in her Cessna. I guess it's time to say goodbye."

"My pa's dead," Andy replied. "He couldn't buy me a ticket."

Bud replied, "I'm talking to Andy Frost, not Andy Hall. Andy, your dad's alive and has been worried about you, as has your mom. It's time to go home."

Bud paused, not sure what Andy would say.

"I have a pa?"

"No, Andy, you have what we call a *dad*. And he misses you, as does your mom. Your last name is Frost, not Hall. You know that. We do better when we face reality, as much as we don't want to sometimes."

Finally, Andy replied, "I take it you've been talking to my parents. But you're right, Sheriff, you're right."

Bud was quiet, waiting for Andy to continue. He soon spoke in a measured voice that had a hint of a Midwestern accent.

"So, you're not going to arrest me?"

"No, Andy. I'm not."

"But you know I was responsible for the oboe player's death, don't you? You're a detective."

"I know you were there, and I think I know what happened. If I'm right, it was an accident. Reece tried to attack you after you played *Boléro*, then accidentally fell off the cliff backwards."

Andy was silent for the longest time, and Bud was actually startled a bit when he started talking again, as he'd gotten caught up in watching the fish jump.

"I'm sorry I misled you when I was telling you about finding the oboe player, Sheriff, but I was scared. Here's what really happened. I heard this guy crying for help, so I went up the back of the cliff and found him. He told me his name was Reece and asked if I was the one they'd sent to get him. I had no idea what he was talking about, and I could see he was in really bad shape."

"Was it dark by then?"

"Almost, but I could still see his face. He looked like death warmed over—I know that sounds insensitive, but it's true. I knew he wasn't going to make it."

"He had an instrument case by him, and he asked me to be sure it got to his sister. He told me her name, but I didn't quite hear it. At that point, he then asked if I would open the case. He wanted to play his oboe. I think that was when he realized he really wasn't going to make it. It was like a last comfort for him."

"So I got it out for him and put it together. He was leaning against a rock, and I handed it to him. I was trying to be helpful, knowing he was soon going to be gone. I didn't know what else to do."

"He started trying to play it, but he was too far gone. All he did was make some really awful sounds. He then started trying to cry, but he wasn't even able to do that, he was so dehydrated."

"He handed me the oboe and asked me to play. He was out of his mind by then, Bud, or at least I thought he was, for most people can't play the oboe. It's a hard instrument. But I could play some from high school, where I played oboe with the band. I knew the theme from *Boléro*—it has a beautiful oboe solo—so I played that for him."

Andy looked back down into the waters, then added, "I've read that people when they're dying sometimes have an unexpected last burst of energy, and it seems that's what happened with him. He managed to stand up, and all of a sudden he was trying to attack me, yelling that I'd stolen his oboe. I handed it back to him just as he lost his balance and tumbled over the edge backwards, the oboe flying off behind him. I later hid the case in the hoodoos so I could somehow get it to his sister, though I had no idea who she was."

"Did you go down to see if he was still alive?"

"I started to, but I could see there was someone camping nearby —they'd just come in. I got really scared, thinking they would accuse me of killing him, so I went back down to the river. I came back the next day and hid the case, and he was gone, as was the guy camping by him. But Bud, he fell a good 50 feet. I've heard that people can't survive after about 40. But do you know what happened to the oboe case?"

"His sister has it now, Andy, so it's all good. I'll tell her what happened when the time's right. She has the oboe, too, or will soon."

Andy asked, "How did you figure out I was there?"

"I wasn't sure until I talked to your mom, and she told me you played oboe in the high-school band, not snare drum. I knew you didn't play snare drum anyway from your reaction earlier when you said you wanted to get back into music. Everyone who plays drums calls it drumming, not music. But after I found out Reece hated *Boléro*, I knew there had to be someone else with him—someone who could play oboe. And you mentioned he had an oboe, yet said you weren't close enough to him to see what he was wearing. A tux is pretty distinctive, so you couldn't have been close enough to know he was carrying an oboe if you couldn't tell he was wearing a tux, and most people would think it was a clarinet anyway. Yet you somehow knew he had an oboe."

Andy asked again, "Are you going to arrest me?"

Bud replied, "No, Andy. That other person camping nearby told me he heard exactly what you just described. I wonder if hearing *Boléro* isn't what sent Reece over the edge—maybe both literally and figuratively."

Andy replied, "I've thought about it a lot since then, and I truly think he was near death anyway. But I still feel really bad about it. I was going to tell you the truth, but I just figured you'd think I was making up some tall yarn, since I'm kind of known for that."

Bud said, "I was thinking a lion scared him over the edge, but something about it just didn't seem right. But Andy, if you're going to tell tall tales, you need to have a good memory to keep the facts straight. It's better to just tell the truth."

Andy wiped his eyes with his sleeve, then said, "My adventure down the river sure didn't turn out like I thought it would. I think I may have gotten a little too much into character. I want to live a life of meaning and purpose, and reading about the adventurous life of Andy Hall struck me. I've always been told I can be too intense. I know I need to come back into the present and make my life into something I want to be doing, not trying to live someone else's life."

He looked into the water, and Bud could tell he was far away. Finally, Andy said, "But it was a good run, don't cha know?"

"It was indeed. Now you can go home and write a book about it— and work on your Scottish accent," Bud laughed.

Andy grinned, then said, "You know, Sheriff, I read about this guy called Tex McClatchy down in Radium. He was a great character who's now gone, and he was referring to future river runners when he said, 'They will never know what we knew, they will never feel what we felt.' He was one of the first river outfitters to offer jet boats and canoe trips to the confluence. His jet boat was named *Major Powell* and his company's still going strong, Tex's Riverways."

"He was right, Andy. We'll never know what it was like on the river back then. He was there from way back in the 1950s."

"It kind of makes me giddy to think that I went down the same river, the same whitewater, that Major Powell and his men went down. It makes me feel special, Bud."

"It does everyone who floats it, Andy. After the Green meets the Colorado, you have some of the most demanding rapids known anywhere. The Colorado's been called the most dangerous river in the world, especially where it goes through Cataract Canyon and then the Grand."

"You know, Bud, while I was down there alone, well, let's just say I don't want to do that again. Every once in awhile I could hear the echoes through the canyons of the cries of those who didn't make it, their boats crashing on the rocks. I was basically a nervous wreck the whole time I was with the crew, worrying about rapids, especially having done so much research and knowing who had died where."

"One can know too much sometimes, Andy. The saying ignorance is bliss can be true."

"I know. I was especially worried about Brown Betty and Cataract Canyon. You know Brown Betty is the first of the whitewater rapids there. It was named after a boat that was eaten by it during the Brown-Stanton expedition of 1889."

"And you're just getting started with Brown Betty, Andy."

"I know, and the Major didn't seem to be a bit worried about it."

"That's because he'd arranged for a jet boat to come down and pick everyone up at Spanish Bottom. He knew that after Cataract it would just be the slackwater of Lake Powell, plus winter was coming and he wanted to get out. He knew they didn't have the experience to run Cataract. They had all the footage they needed to get financial backing at that point."

"Except they forgot about me. But what footage and backing?"

"The Major got a big fine for commercial filming in a national park with no permit. He told the park rangers he was making a pilot to try to get funding for a documentary re-enactment of Powell's journey. I called them today about the boats to see if they knew what was going on. You didn't know about the movie?"

Andy looked shocked. "No!"

Bud continued. "It would explain the fellows I saw lurking out of sight of everyone the first day I saw you all down on the river. I think the Major was trying to capture the reality of it and thereby didn't tell anyone they were filming. They had a couple of guys coming down on a raft after you guys, filming on the sly."

"That explains a few things. It's not very ethical and makes me glad I did a lot of serious cussing. That'll increase his editing costs."

"He'll have to get permission waivers from all of you in order to use it anyway. I'm surprised he didn't tell you what was going on."

"He told us that we were doing a re-enactment and it was very important to stay in character. That's all he talked about the whole time, staying in character."

"That's because they were filming it," Bud replied.

"We knew there were two guys following us in a raft, but the Major just said they were the sweep boat, whatever that is."

Bud asked, "Why weren't those two also at Spanish Bottom?"

"I saw their raft on a trailer going up the Mineral Bottom Road. They took out there. I think they were either finished or fed up."

Bud asked, "How did you get the job, anyway?"

"It was in a classified ad. And I know I won't get paid now. And I'll never forgive the Major for running me off, then not even waiting for me when they all went out of the canyon on the jet boat."

"He probably had no idea where you were and didn't realize there was a trail out of Spanish Bottom. It's the only place where there *is* a trail out of the canyon."

"I was up at the Dollhouse. But I wonder why the jet boat didn't take all the dories out when they got the Major and everyone?"

"The Major told the ranger they were planning on coming back.

Hauling four wooden dories out plus a bunch of people would overload the boat, so they made arrangements for a couple of boats to come in later, but then the weather interfered, and the park rangers got there first."

"And gave me a fine. I didn't even do anything. You don't need a permit to run the Green. It makes as much sense as government cheese."

"The ranger told me you got a fine for being part of the illegal filming, Andy, not for running the Green."

"I got fined for doing something I didn't even know I was doing," Andy said in disgust, looking again into the dark waters below. "And some Major. He was just a history buff from Rapid City, not a real Major."

Bud said, "I need to get back to work. I hope you have a good flight home. I know your parents are anxious to see you."

"I'll be back, Bud. You know, Tex McClatchy also said something else that struck me. He said, 'Find a place you like and figure out how to live there.' I'm going to apply to Tex's Riverways as an apprentice river guide next spring."

"What about all those spooky voices you heard on the river?" Bud asked.

Andy laughed. "I'll get used to them, plus I won't be alone. But Bud, Howie gave me this slip of paper last night at the party. We'd been talking earlier. It's a quote from *The Wind in the Willows*."

He handed Bud the paper.

Take the Adventure, heed the call, now ere the irrevocable moment passes! 'Tis but a banging of the door behind you, a blithesome step forward, and you are out of the old life and into the new!

"That's great, Andy." Bud said, handing it back.

Andy replied, "I know I can run those rapids with a little experience under my belt."

"Sounds fantastic. But Andy, can I ask how old you are?"

"Twenty-two," he replied, then seeing Bud frown, said, "Eighteen."

"Not even old enough to drink hard liquor," Bud said, then added,

"Andy, take the adventure, but maybe spend a little more time at home with your folks while you can. You have your whole life ahead of you. But be sure to look me up when you come back."

"Thanks, Bud, I will. I'll never forget you."

"Same, Andy."

They stood awhile watching the heron, then turned and walked back across the bridge and on to better things.

~

I f you enjoyed this book, join Bud in his new book, *A Slice of Life in Watermelon Town*.

Join Sheriff Bud Shumway in this compilation of his best photos, each accompanied by his descriptions of the what and where and how, which will leave you laughing or shaking your head, but never bored. And you'll feel right at home in this enjoyable slice of Bud's life as you ride along on this personal tour of his little town of Green River, Utah, AKA Watermelon Town, which sits right smack in the middle of what he calls the Big Empty, a geologic wonderland perfect for his wanderings with his dogs while taking photos.

"My wife says I'm a mystery magnet," Bud says. "She's a real go-getter who collects the best of my photos each year to make a 'Best of Bud' calendar for friends and family. She wanted me to write about some of my experiences, so here they are."

If you've read any of the Bud Shumway Mystery Series, you're familiar with Sheriff Bud and his mellow laid-back outlook while dealing with the numerous whacky and mystifying crimes that seem to follow him around.

Haven't read the books? It's not necessary, as you can come along anyway for a look into one of America's most unique towns. You'll be glad you did, for who doesn't need a little humor and happiness in these trying times? And maybe Bud's mellow attitude will help arm you for the craziness in your own life, as one reviewer claimed the books had done for her. Come join Bud for a slice of life in Watermelon Town, the America we all want to be a part of.

ABOUT THE AUTHOR

Chinle Miller writes from southeastern Utah and western Colorado, where she spends most of her time wandering with her dogs. She has an A.S. in Geology, a B.A. in Anthropology, and an M.A. in Linguistics.

If you enjoyed this book, you'll also enjoy the other books in the Bud Shumway mystery series:

The Ghost Rock Cafe
The Slickrock Cafe
The Paradox Cafe
The No Delay Cafe
The Silver Spur Cafe
The Ice House Cafe
The Rattlesnake Cafe
The Beartooth Cafe
The Melon Rind Cafe
The Cessna Cafe
The Klondike Cafe
The Yellow Cat Cafe
The Swiftcurrent Cafe
The Sunnyside Cafe

The Temple Mountain Cafe is the fifteenth book in the series.

And don't miss *Desert Rats: Adventures in the American Outback, Uranium Daughter, Wandering off the Map,* and *The Impossibility of Loneliness,* also by Chinle Miller.

And if you enjoy Bigfoot stories, you'll love *Rusty Wilson's Bigfoot Campfire Stories* and his many other Bigfoot books, as well as his popular *Chasing After Bigfoot: My Search for North America's Most Elusive Creature*.

Other offerings from Yellow Cat Publishing include an RV series by RV expert Sunny Skye, which includes *Living the Simple RV Life, The Truth about the RV Life,* and *RVing with Pets,* as well as *Tales of a Campground Host.* And don't forget to check out the books by Sunny's friend, Bob Davidson: *On the Road with Joe* and *Any Road, USA.* And finally, you'll love Roger Dean Miller's comedy thriller, *Bombing Hoffman.*

www.ingramcontent.com/pod-product-compliance
Lightning Source LLC
Chambersburg PA
CBHW071433260626
47170CB00008B/2696